1 3 JUN 2014

2 1 JAN 2017

GW00586706

i0

30127 06791747 1

A MINIATURE MURDER MYSTERY

Sheila Fyffe went to Mark Preston out of spite, and he took the case reluctantly. The verdict on Honoria Lockhart was accidental death, and there was no reason why anyone should want to murder her. An elderly woman of modest means, she lived quietly, concentrating on her hobby of copying old manuscripts.

Her younger husband had nothing to gain. Honoria's death brought him unwelcome attention, and also left him homeless. The only other relative was an even older sister.

Preston brightened up when he met the lawyer lady, Hortense Mulligan, and became positively enthusiastic with the advent of night-club singer Juliet Freeman.

But the next death was unquestionably murder, and the wrong people would suffer unless Preston solved the puzzle.

A MINIATURE MURDER MYSTERY

Peter Chambers

·BLACK·
DAGGER
·CRIME·

First published 1982
by
Robert Hale Ltd

This edition 2006 by BBC Audiobooks Ltd
published by arrangement with
the author

ISBN 10: 1 4056 8549 2
ISBN 13: 978 1 405 68549 8

British Library Cataloguing in Publication Data available

Printed and bound in Great Britain by
Antony Rowe Ltd., Chippenham, Wiltshire

ONE

No one could accuse Mrs Sheila Fyffe of pussyfooting around. When that lady had a question to ask, she asked it. Like the one she had just asked me.

'Do you do murders?'

As an opening gambit, it lacked finesse. I was accustomed to some peculiar conversations. Mine is a highly confidential business, and that was often fortunate for the clients. Some of the things I'd heard in my office would make your hair stand on end. Usually though, they tend to hum and haw before they get to the point. A little chat about the weather, last night's baseball, nuclear disarmament. Anything, just so it keeps them off that vital subject which brought them to me in the first place.

Sheila Fyffe was not of their number.

A thin, angular woman, of fifty plus, she had a worry-lined face beneath the deep California tan. Elusive eyes of pale blue. Now they were looking at you, now they weren't, almost as though prolonged direct contact might damage them in some way.

Did I do murders?

The short answer to that would have to be 'no'. I couldn't even redirect her to a reputable firm who could be relied on to give satisfaction in that field. But I wasn't going to give the short answer. I had a feeling that if I did, she would be up and gone, and I wouldn't even get to know the vital details. Like, for instance, who was the victim of her choice, how much would it pay? Background stuff like that. I was also a mite curious to know whether someone might have recommended me for the job. A man likes to know who his friends are.

'Well now, Mrs Fyffe,' I replied, picking my words with care. 'I wonder if you would mind elaborating on that just a little?'

'Ah. Yes. Well, I don't know much about these things, you see. I seem to remember hearing somewhere that people in your line of business tend to specialise. Some concentrate on divorce work, I believe. Some deal with industrial espionage. That kind of thing, I don't know whether you might be one of those. Because, if you are, we can terminate the conversation at once. I need someone who undertakes murders.'

It was getting better. The lady could have chosen her words more closely, even now, but I thought I knew what she intended to say. It wasn't the commission of murder that was on offer. It was the investigation of one.

'Well,' I hedged, 'I have sometimes become involved in cases of murder, but not in competition with the police, you understand. We have a very fine homicide department here in Monkton City, and I'll be glad to give you the name of the officer in charge. Unless they are already at work on the case, that is.'

She shook her head firmly.

'Useless, they will do nothing. According to them,

6

there's nothing they can do. Practically threw me out. Man named Rourke. Do you know him?'

I knew him. Captain of Detectives, so-called, but only paid in the rank of lieutenant, because of our parsimonious civil purse operators. John Rourke, for all our little differences of opinion, was an efficient and committed officer. If he didn't feel he could help my visitor, I doubted whether there was much I could do.

'Mr Rourke is a very able man,' I told her, 'with all the resources of a large department behind him. I am only one man. What makes you think I can help you.'

She sniffed.

'Don't know whether you can. Won't know until you try. That person Rourke won't even try.'

'Ah. Perhaps if you could let me have a few details about the – um – murder.'

My hesitation over the word did not escape her. The pale eyes held me for a moment, then slid away.

'You sound like that Rourke already,' she observed, 'and you haven't even heard the details yet. At least he went that far.'

'No, no,' I hastened to contradict. 'I am most interested, really. Please let me hear the story.'

Satisfied that I had been properly chastened, she composed herself, and began to deliver.

'The deceased was my dear friend and one-time employer, Honoria Parker. Did you want to write that down?'

What sounded like a question was really a command. People were clearly expected to take notes, and I was the

7

only people present. Sliding open a drawer, I produced one notepad, immaculate, and one pencil, sharp. I wrote down the name, Honoria Parker, and waited for more.

'That is her correct name, you understand. The name by which she was known and respected for over fifty years. At the time of her – death, she had another name.'

Mrs Fyffe paused, and I thought it was a signal, so I picked up the pencil again. Silence.

'This other name?' I queried. 'I'm going to need it, surely?'

There was a tight head movement opposite.

'Lockhart. She was married to this Lockhart creature. It was he who killed her, of course.'

Of course.

'I take it the lady was married rather late in life?'

'She was fifty-nine years old when the so-called ceremony was performed. The law should prevent this kind of thing from happening in the first place.' I wrote down 'age fifty-nine' and my prospective client watched anxiously.

'What's that you're writing?'

'Just as well to have a note of the lady's age,' I explained.

'I haven't told you that yet,' she snapped.

'But you said—'

'I said she was fifty-nine when they were married. She didn't die until a little over a year later. Fourteen months in fact. Sixty – that's how old she was.'

I corrected the figure. We were coming along fine, I reflected. In the space of only ten minutes I had been able to learn not only the name of the dead woman, but also her age. By Thanksgiving there wouldn't be much about her that I didn't know.

'And Mr Lockhart?' I prompted. 'Would you know his first name, and his age if possible?'

'Calls himself Franklin. Ought to be a law about that, too. Person like him, using the same name as dear Mr Roosevelt. As to his age, he says he's thirty-five.'

That was the most telling piece of information I'd had so far, and it tempted me to think I now had the whole story.

Honoria Parker, probably a woman of some substance, had been conned into marriage by a man twenty-five years her junior. That cut out Sheila Fyffe, previously housekeeper or companion or the like. Honoria later died, Lockhart scooped up his winnings, and Mrs Fyffe was howling for blood. I wouldn't have any figures as to how many times a day this particular scenario was enacted in the state of California, but it was a very commonplace story. There are always refinements, naturally. I waited to hear them.

'You're not saying anything,' she said peremptorily.

'It's a little early for me to say much,' I replied reasonably. 'In this kind of work, a man learns not to jump to hasty conclusions. Much better to get all the facts first. How did Mrs Lockhart come to meet her death?'

'Poison,' was the firm reply. 'She was poisoned.'

'Poison,' I repeated, 'and yet, if I understand you, the police are taking no action.'

9

'Oh well,' she dismissed, 'they say it was an accidental overdose. That's what they say. You'd think they'd take more trouble.'

'An overdose? Then the lady was taking some kind of drug? Would that have been for some special condition?'

'No, no. Sleeping pills, nothing more. She hadn't been sleeping well for some time. A body can scarcely wonder, what with being married to that creature and all.'

I nodded politely.

'So, it would seem that Mrs Lockhart, somehow or other, took more of these sedatives than she ought, and died as a result.'

'You haven't heard the best bit yet,' she clipped, from a tight line of mouth. 'They say she probably didn't realise what she was doing, because of all the alcohol in her system.'

The story was becoming more depressingly familiar as it progressed. The papers carry stories every day about people dying in precisely the circumstances described by Mrs Fyffe. If there was murder here, it was going to be a tough one to prove. I ought to have realised that, the moment she told me John Rourke had not been interested.

'Why do you say that is the best bit, Mrs Fyffe?'

There was triumph on her face now. Somebody was listening at last. Someone who would perhaps comprehend the truth behind what she was saying.

'The idea of Honoria with alcohol in her system is plain ridiculous,' she explained. 'One glass of wine at

Christmas was her annual intake. Does that sound to you like a person who'd make drunken mistakes? Well, does it?'

I had to admit that it didn't, and I said so. But I had to add something else.

'But still, whatever the lady's normal habits may have been, there can be no doubt the alcohol was in her system. Medical examiners don't make mistakes about things like that. We may not know the reason for it, but Mrs Lockhart must have been drinking on that day. You can't fake scientific evidence of that kind.'

'Oh, I realise all that,' she scoffed. 'I'm not trying to contradict what the doctors say. What I'm telling you is that it's just totally out of character. Honoria isn't – wasn't – a drinking woman, and that's all there is to it.'

I looked at her helplessly.

'Then how do you explain it?'

'Forced on her,' she asserted. 'He must have forced it on her, somehow. Don't ask me how, because I don't know. Anyway, that's your job. Or it will be, if you decide to help me. You will, won't you?'

Some of the confidence had gone from her manner now. She was a worried and anxious woman, looking desperately for support.

'Mrs Fyffe, I must tell you that I'm not very hopeful about this. No, hear me out' – as she seemed about to interrupt – 'I'm not saying I won't try. I'll ask a few questions, get some facts together, and then decide if it's worth going on with. I'm an expensive man to hire, and I will not take money under false pretenses. It wouldn't be

11

difficult to spin this out for a week, or even two. That would cost you a great deal of money, and it might all be for nothing. I don't work that way. If I don't find something worth chasing within forty-eight hours, I will tell you, and we'll call it a day. Is that agreeable?'

'But you will try?'

'For forty-eight hours, yes. Before I start though, I'm going to need a lot more information.'

She nodded her agreement, and we began.

Honoria had lived in a ranch-style bungalow out on Montenero Drive. Sheila Fyffe's description was 'neat', but what she meant was small. I knew the district, and it was an area where the better-paid artisans set up house. Small properties, well cared-for, and each with a two-year old car parked carefully alongside the square of shaved grass referred to as the lawn. An area of medium incomes and high principles, where people kept themselves to themselves, but always with a keen eye to neighbouring activities.

The dead woman had fitted well into the surroundings. She had no need to work, thanks to a small private income from the estate of her late father. At the mention of money, my interest perked up.

'You wouldn't have any idea of how much was involved?' I asked.

'She never told me, but it was always enough. Honoria lived very quietly, you see. Didn't go out much, and so her expenses were not high.'

'Quite. What would happen to that income after her death?'

12

Sheila Fyffe's eyes were lively at the question. 'Got you interested, haven't I? That's something I wouldn't know. You'd have to ask the lawyers about that. It would be nice for Mr Franklin Lockhart, if it should pass to him, now wouldn't it?'

'It would certainly be interesting,' I agreed. 'Please go on.'

Mrs Fyffe, it transpired, had been widowed some five years previously. In her new state she was comfortably placed financially, but, being childless, she tired quickly of living alone. She knew Honoria slightly, from marketing trips and so forth, and was aware that she too was now alone in the house. It appeared that there had been another woman living with her, as a kind of companion. The woman's sister-in-law had died suddenly, leaving several children to be cared for, which was a task her bereaved brother could not cope with. The companion decided to leave Honoria, and keep house for her brother. The upshot of it all was that Sheila Fyffe moved in with Honoria, an arrangement which suited both of them very well.

'Until he turned up, that is.'

'Mr Lockhart,' I mused. 'Yes. Please tell me about that.'

There wasn't a lot she knew. Honoria suddenly became rather secretive about her movements, but Mrs Fyffe wasn't too concerned. She simply thought that her friend was going through some emotional disturbance of her own, and would snap out of it, given time. It had been quite a shock when Honoria suddenly announced

13

that she intended to get married, and that Sheila would have to make new arrangements.

'It must have been very upsetting,' I condoled.

'Not at first,' she denied. 'It would involve me in some upheaval, of course, but I was very pleased for my friend. Until I saw him, that is. I could tell his sort right off.'

'What sort would that be, Mrs Fyffe?'

'Slicker type,' she retorted primly. 'Smart alec. You know? Fancy haircuts and bow ties. That kind.'

'Ah yes,' I said gravely.

Clearly, if the world was ever to be safe for democracy, the first logical step must be to deport everyone with a fancy haircut, or a bow tie. It would certainly relieve traffic congestion, for a start. I made a mental note that there must be no bow tie whenever I ran across my new client.

'So you had to move out,' I prompted.

'Couldn't get out fast enough, once it was all decided,' she assured me. 'Not that I didn't try to talk her out of it, mind. We almost came to a quarrel, but I wouldn't give him that satisfaction.'

'Him?'

'Certainly,' she sniffed. 'Nothing he would have liked better than to have her old friend shown the door. He didn't want me around. Made that quite clear.'

'But you left amicably, in the end?' I pressed.

'Oh yes. Even gave them a wedding present. I hope I know how to behave. When I think of what I was leaving her to, I just wish I hadn't gone at all. Makes me feel responsible. If only I'd stuck to my guns, that poor dear soul might have been alive today.'

Mrs Fyffe dived into her handbag, and produced a handkerchief. For a moment I was afraid she might break down, but two heavy intakes of breath restored her composure.

'I don't think there's any justification for you to blame yourself,' I soothed. 'After all, the lady was the one who made the original decision. To get married, I mean. She was in full health, I take it?'

'If you are asking me whether Honoria was not very strong mentally, I have to refute that. Strong as an ox, mind and body.'

I didn't care for the analogy too well. When it comes to the I.Q. ratings, the ox is not among the front runners. But I knew what she was trying to say. Honoria Lockhart was as sane as you or me.

'Do you happen to know whether there was a will?'

My visitor shook her head.

'I wouldn't know that. Not for certain. He says there is, but that could have been just to spite me.'

'Mr Lockhart? You asked him whether there was a will?'

There must have been something in my tone which produced the look of affront she gave me.

'Certainly not. What kind of question is that?'

'But you said—' I began.

'I said he told me. That is not the same thing as one having asked him. The very idea.'

In earlier times, Mrs Fyffe would be wearing starched

15

clothes, and the starch would be crackling at that moment. I would have to come again, from another direction.

'When did you actually see Mr Lockhart?'

'After the funeral, of course. I went out to the house, and asked could I have one of the drawings. Just a keepsake, that's all. He wouldn't even concede me that. One, that was all I asked for, out of hundreds. But oh no, not from that man. It all depended on what Honoria's will said, that's what he told me. I could ask again, in a couple of days. He knew I wouldn't, naturally. I don't go crawling to people.'

This was the first I'd heard about any drawings. It sounded like a point worth pursuing.

'Was she a collector, then, your friend?'

She looked puzzled for a moment, then understanding dawned.

'Oh, you mean did she collect drawings? No. They weren't that kind. Honoria did them all herself. Not proper drawings, I don't mean. Not like people or sunsets, or the like. It was her hobby, you see. There's a word for it. Cali something. I always say callisthenics, but that isn't it.'

'Could it be caligraphy?' I prompted.

She nodded eagerly.

'That's it. Caligraphy. Never can recall that word. Funny kind of hobby. But she did beautiful work. Had to have special brushes, and paints and all. Had to write all over to get the materials. Amsterdam, Brussels, London England. She would spend days, doing just one little

16

page. I always admired her work. You'd think he could have spared me just one. Not much to ask.'

I put on my understanding look.

'Well, I may find it necessary to talk to Mr Lockhart. If you like, I could mention it.'

'Oh, would you?' She was almost animated. 'I'd be so grateful. I certainly wouldn't ask him myself, not a second time. He may not find it so easy to refuse a man.'

'Well, no harm in asking,' I said reassuringly. 'Is there anyone else I ought to see? Any other friends? I gather there are no relatives.'

'Oh yes, there's the sister. But she couldn't tell you much.'

'Ah.' This was the first mention of a sister. 'Perhaps I could just ask you about her?'

That mouth was tight again.

'Can't tell you much. Never met her myself. They didn't get on, you see. The other one, Rowena, she's the one Lockhart ought to have married, if it was money he wanted. Wealthy woman, that one, not that it does her much good. She's practically one of those recluses. Lives in a big old house, out at the Heights. Not a young woman, of course. Over seventy by now. She came to the funeral though, I'll say that for her. All in black, she was. Made quite an impression, I can tell you. Took me back, to tell you the truth. You don't see much by way of black at funerals these days. Reminded me of my own dear mother, with the veils and everything.'

Anxious to avoid a recall session of past funerals, I asked quickly.

17

'Would you happen to have the sister's address?'

'No, I wouldn't know that. Easy enough to find, I imagine. Can't be too many people over at the Heights named Rowena Parker.'

This was delivered in a tone suggesting that a big detective ought to have been able to work it out for himself. The interview had lasted long enough, I decided.

'Well, I don't think I need take up any more of your time, Mrs Fyffe,' I smiled. 'I'll let you know if anything develops, though I must repeat what I said at the beginning. I'm not very hopeful of getting results.'

'Understood. But at least I will know that I tried. One can only try.'

With which unctuous delivery she went away.

I sat and stared at my meagre notes, thinking. It was all a pointless exercise, of course. There was nothing here for me. All I could do would be to tramp around, bang on a few doors, make out some kind of report. Mrs Fyffe wanted some action, and was paying me to provide it. Well, the least I could do was not to waste time. Her time.

Tearing off the top sheet of notepaper, I shoved it in my pocket, and headed for the outside world.

18

TWO

In Monkton City we have many fine public buildings. Our City Hall is the envy of many a State Capital, and when it comes to parks and gardens, we are up there with the front runners. The civic pride extends even to the prison system. Many an article has appeared in national magazines, about the humane treatment afforded to offenders. Not for us the six-to-a-cell, the sweat-shop workrooms, the cramped facilities. Many an ex-prisoner will tell you that the conditions inside are several jumps ahead of his normal living surroundings.

Of course the public purse is not a bottomless pit. There is a limit to what can be done, even in the most enlightened communities. Some things have to wait their turn, especially with inner city land values the way they are. One of the places still waiting its turn is Police Headquarters. Not forgotten, mark you, just waiting. Mayor Blanks said only last year that people need not think the city administration was unaware of the trying circumstances under which our police are working. This was a matter under constant review, and was a top priority with the planners. It was comforting to read what he'd said, because it was confirmation of what Mayor Hanks had said five years ago, and Mayor Stranks had said five years before that. This shows

19

consistent thinking, which is what the public wants from top officials.

In the meantime, pending these imminent great changes, the boys in blue carry on protecting the public from the same shamble of buildings, donated with a great fanfare in 1910. Those were the days when that great sheriff Fighting Tom Forrest ran the whole shebang with six deputies. Nothing was too good for that dedicated band, and the stables in which their horses lived would have done credit to a pedigree racehorse trainer. No cattle rustler was safe then, no renegade Indians could hope to evade those vigilant men. In fact, they seem to have done the job so well that there is almost no cattle-rustling any more, and no one can remember the last time a renegade started whooping it up. But crime marches on, and the police along with it, and those airy spacious quarters allotted to the six deputies, plus horses, still accommodate the guardians of the peace. There are many 'temporary' extensions of course, plus Quonsett huts on all sides, and some of the partitioning work is little short of genius. If headquarters occupied some other function, such as housing the homeless, or as a refugee centre, the public outcry would be heard clear across the continent. But nobody is going to set up a committee to support the police. They are a civic responsibility, a city hall matter, and, in any case, Mayor Blanks had said only last year—

I managed to find a space to park the car, and marched up the worn steps leading into the main building. The sergeant doing desk duty eyed me gravely as I approached.

'Well, well, it's Mr Preston, ain't it? Conscience finally got you down, huh? I'll have somebody come and take your statement.'

'Hallo Mac. What's the charge?'

He raised his eyebrows in mock affront.

'I won't know that till we get your confession. Don't you worry about it. Kinda stuff you pull, we oughta be able to fix you up with a nice ten to twenty.'

I nodded.

'Just so I don't have to spend it in these lovely surroundings.'

Mac squinted at me.

'Listen, this is only temporary. Matter of fact, this place don't conform to the public health regulations. There was a guy here, just a few weeks back, checking around. Told me so himself. Guess that'll stir things up, huh, wouldn't you say?'

'Young man, was he?'

'That's right, fair hair with glasses. You know him?'

I didn't know him. All I knew was that only a young man would pass on that kind of information. He probably thought, with his brand new diploma, that his report would produce some instant action. But the report would go to older men, men who knew the system. They would pat him on the head, and transfer him to something more profitable.

'No, I don't think so. Is Rourke around?'

He consulted a sheet which lay by his elbow.

'Upstairs,' he grunted. 'You'll have to walk. Elevator's on the blink again.'

Nodding my thanks, I headed for the rickety stairway. I always walked. Nothing but brute force would have got me inside that death trap elevator.

The Homicide Bureau occupies rooms on the third floor. One door is half-panelled in opaque glass. The glass is opaque so that visitors can't see through it. The accumulated dirt performs the same function for the daylight. The legend, almost visible to the naked eye, reads 'J. Rourke, Captain of Detectives'. I knocked lightly, and went inside. The familiar grizzled head was bent over some papers.

'Can it wait?' he growled. 'I'm pretty busy right now.'

'You carry on,' I told him. 'I'll just stand here and admire the furniture.'

He looked up quickly at the sound of my voice, and a pained look came over the lined face.

'Oh no,' he protested. 'You I don't deserve. Tell me where I went wrong.'

'Nice to see you too, John,' I assured him. 'Been a long time. How are things?'

Leaning back, he rested his arms on the battered desk top.

'How're things?' he echoed. 'I'll tell you how're things. Gil Randall is away sick. They sent Schultz away on some fancy pants course, to teach him how to be a police officer. They give me one kid, about twelve years old, to cover for these able and experienced men. I have three non-natural causes to investigate, plus a double shooting down in the harbor last night. That's how're things.'

Randall was Rourke's number two, and Schultz was a key man on the squad. I didn't envy the twelve year old substitute.

'That's too bad, John,' I clucked. 'What's with Randall, is it serious?'

'Nah,' he denied, 'It's some throat thing. Should clear up in a few days, but the doc says he can't work in this atmosphere. Can you imagine?'

Sliding open a green pack, he removed one of his poisonous little Spanish cigars and set fire to it. A pungent yellow cloud rose around his head. Maybe the doctor had a point.

'OK to sit down?'

I pointed to the visitors' chair, a dangerous wooden contraption which was designed for maximum discomfort.

'Why not?' he waved expansively. 'Come one, come all, that's what I say. There's nothing for me to do here all day. Glad of a chat with every passing horse-thief. How's trade?'

'Things are a little slow at the moment,' I told him. 'But there is one little matter I'd like to discuss.'

He looked concerned.

'You know I don't buy stolen horses. Besides, they leave hoofmarks on the lawn.'

'This is something different. I think you may have been talking with a Mrs Sheila Fyffe. About the recent death of one Honoria Lockhart.'

Several of the furrows on his brow moved closer

23

together.

'Wait a minute. Was this the overdose case? Lady had a few drinks and swallowed too many pills?'

'That's the one,' I confirmed.

'I remember. This other woman, the friend, she wanted me to lock up the husband.' His face tightened. 'Yeah, I do remember now. This Mrs – Fyffe, did you say? – Right, Mrs Fyffe, she started raising all kinds of hallelujah. I tried to be reasonable with her, but she wasn't in the business of listening. She was in the business of telling, and I was the one got told. Practically accused me of covering up a homicide. Can you imagine?'

I could imagine Mrs Fyffe doing precisely that. I could also imagine Rourke's reaction.

'That's the lady,' I said sadly. 'Kind of high-spirited. She got a little rough with me, too.'

He peered at me from folded lids.

'Why would she do that?'

'Because I told her if the bureau couldn't help her, I didn't see that I could be much use.'

'You told her that?'

'Exact words.'

'H'm.'

He slid a pencil around between his fingers. It looked like a kitchen match in those gnarled hands.

'So why are you here?'

'She insisted that I should poke around, see if I could dig something up. I told her it was a waste of money. She said it was her money, and that was one I couldn't argue.'

The pencil made a flat clicking sound as he laid it on the desk top.

'Why are you telling me all this?'

'Courtesy of the trade,' I replied smoothly. 'Plus, I wanted you to know where I stand. It wouldn't do for you to hear from somebody else that I was trying to open up a file you'd already closed. You might even think I was meddling in police business.'

'Huh,' he snorted. 'That is what you spend your day doing nothing else but. What do you hope to find?'

'Nothing,' I admitted. 'I propose to see a few people, ask a lot of questions, make up a nice report, and send the lady a bill.'

'Good,' he decided, to my relief. 'Only, make it a lot of people and a big report, with a bill to match. Maybe it'll teach people there's no percentage in hiring private policemen. What do you know about this case, if it is a case?'

'Only what she told me. You're sure to know a lot more. That's another reason I'm here.'

'Oh it is, is it? You think I'm going to do your work for you?'

'Not at all,' I denied. 'It's just a favor between old friends. Besides, there will be people I don't need to see, because you've already done it. We wouldn't want the idea getting around that maybe there is some crime here after all, and maybe the department missed something.'

He glowered across, and I gave him my open-faced look of sweet innocence.

'Are you leaning on me, Preston?'

'Certainly not,' I disclaimed. 'The very idea. What

25

I'm offering here is one hundred per cent cooperation. The idea is, if I come up with something, I get back to you first. The outside world doesn't know you closed the file. For all they know, you're digging away in the background the whole time. If anything crops up, you will know it, and you can decide what to do about it. Cooperation, see?'

He rubbed his thumb across a rasping chin, thinking over what I'd said. Then he jabbed the thumb down on the buzzer.

'Wait till you see this.'

The door opened and a young man came in, almost on the run. He had a smooth unlined faced and clear blue eyes beneath a short-cropped thatch of blond hair. Six feet two and gangly, he was bursting to be of service. He didn't look at me. His eyes were all for the fearsome Rourke.

'Yessir, captain?'

'It's lieutenant, how many more times,' grumbled his chief. 'This here is Mr Mark Preston. He's what they call a private investigator. Take a good look at him. You may have to lock him up one of these days. This, Mr Preston, is Probationer Detective Henry Larsen.'

The youngster looked me over, puzzlement plain on his face. He was having his problems, adjusting to Rourke's technique.

'Hallo Henry,' I grinned.

'Mr Preston,' he acknowledged, swallowing.

He wasn't quite certain whether he was supposed to smile, or show me his rubber truncheon.

Rourke rescued him.

'We had an Accidental last week. Female. Name of Lockhart. See if you can dig it up some time. Let's say, by the time I count twenty.'

Larsen went out on the run.

'Seems like a nice enough boy,' I offered.

'Boy is right,' grumbled the Irishman. 'I'm short two men, so they send me one apprentice. What kind of arithmetic is that? I tell you, Preston, if the crooks in this city knew what went on in this office, they'd be out in the street, gunning each other down. Who's to stop 'em, that's what I want to know?'

There was a pounding of feet outside, and the new recruit came in at the double. He was carrying a slim brown-colored file, which he placed carefully in front of his chief.

'This is the one cap – lieutenant,' he announced.

Rourke picked it up, inspected the little reference sticker, opened it and peered inside.

'So it is.' Then he glared at the expectant Larsen. 'Did you want something?'

'No, sir.'

'Then don't stand there, watching me work. Get out and do some of your own. I seem to recall there's still some unsolved crime in this metropolis of ours. Come back here when it's all cleared up.'

Henry nodded, and went out like a jet.

'That should hold him for the next twenty years,' I suggested.

'Thirty. It's taken me that long already, and things are just as bad as when I started,' was the growled reply. 'It's

27

like painting the Golden Gate Bridge. By the time you get to the end, you have to go back and start over. Now then, what have we here?'

What we had here was a thin sheaf of papers. Over the years, I had acquired some skill in reading upside-down. Unfortunately for me, Rourke was aware of it. He held the papers so that I couldn't apply the technique, and skimmed quickly through them.

'Well, it's as I remembered. The woman had a few drinks, then she took more sleeping pills than she ought to. Very ordinary case. I'll get another one, just like it, before the week is out.'

'She wasn't a drinking woman. Does that put a question in your mind?'

He shook his head.

'No way. If anything, it makes it easier to understand. It's often people who don't drink who get themselves in trouble when they try. They can't handle the stuff, the system isn't used to it. Take this Mrs Lockhart. Maybe she had something to celebrate. Or, maybe she just thought she'd try a little experiment. Maybe she was unhappy, because she couldn't sleep. Who knows? The fact is, the booze was in the system when the coroner's people worked on her. I only deal in facts.'

'You didn't suspect the husband may have had something to do with it?'

'No, why would I do that?'

'Because you're a careful man, and because I know you,' I replied. 'This Lockhart was twenty odd years younger than the dead woman. It wouldn't be the first time a man in that situation bumped off his wife, so he could collect the estate.'

'Oh dear me,' he mocked. 'I hadn't considered that possibility. You're getting confused, Preston. The one who is new to the police business is Larsen. This is Rourke you're talking to.'

'And?'

'And my nasty old mind put me on to this Lockhart the minute I read the report. Trouble is, there's no motive. The estate, as you call it, amounts to a few hundred dollars.'

'But the house,' I protested. 'That has to be worth thirty thousand plus. Wouldn't you call that a motive?'

'Yes, I would,' he agreed. 'But he don't get the house. Mrs Lockhart didn't own it. She just lived there.'

That was unexpected news. Clearly, the dead woman hadn't told her dear friend Mrs Fyffe all the facts.

'I didn't know that,' I confessed. 'But she had a private income, I'm told. What becomes of that?'

'Ceased on her death,' he informed me with quiet triumph. 'You got any more bright ideas? Jewellery, perhaps? A secret stock of Rembrandt paintings? Forget 'em. There was nothing. Believe me, I didn't like the smell of this, any more than you do. I had Gil Randall sniff around, before he went sick. Sergeant Randall, as you may have observed over the years, is not the man to miss very much. There wasn't a thing he could find. In my book, that means there wasn't anything to be found.'

I couldn't argue with that. Randall was a very thorough and painstaking man, as I'd learned to my cost many times in the past.

'I'm beginning to think I'm wasting my time,' I said, half to myself.

Rourke beamed with pleasure.

'That's the most encouraging thing you've said so far.' He sounded almost cheerful. 'Well, I guess that's it, huh? Any time you need a few pointers about methods of investigation, and so forth, don't hesitate to drop in. We aim to serve.'

'Nice of you,' I acknowledged. 'Would you mind telling me the name of the lawyer who handled this?'

'You mean you're going on with it?'

'I'm being paid, John,' I explained. 'After what you told me, I don't expect to get anywhere. But my client has the right to know that I made some kind of investigation.'

'Well,' he muttered, 'I guess you have to earn a living, Lord knows why. Got the name of the firm here, someplace. Yup, here it is. Prentiss and Prentiss. You know 'em?'

I searched around my memory, but nothing happened.

'There are so many,' I replied. 'New people, are they?'

Rourke ground out the remains of his cigar. I watched thankfully as the last spiral of smoke eddied up to take its place in the atmosphere. Randall's doctor, I reflected, knew a thing or two.

'New, you say? Well yes, I guess some people would say that. Kind of new. They certainly weren't here when the Spanish came.'

I was being ribbed. The Spanish had come in the late sixteenth century.

'In fact,' continued Rourke, 'I doubt whether the family has been here a hundred years all told. No, I would doubt it. You'd have to ask Mr Prentiss Junior.'

'That'll be the son,' I nodded.

'Wrong,' he contradicted. 'That'll be the father. Mr Prentiss Senior died about twenty years ago. Mr Prentiss Junior, oh yes, they still call him that, must be pushing around seventy years old.'

Nearly seventy. I was beginning to feel hemmed in by old age. Surely there had to be somebody involved in this case who came into a lower age bracket? Oh, of course, I remembered. There was Franklin Lockhart. At that moment I felt almost grateful to him. At least he was named after the younger Roosevelt. It could have been Theodore.

'Sounds like a live wire outfit,' I observed. 'I'd better make a note of the address. Which of your coroners did the autopsy?'

Rourke frowned, turning over paper.

'Man called Humbold. Jack Humbold. Know him?'

I knew him. Humbold wasn't yet thirty years old. He must have got on to the case by mistake.

'I know him,' I confirmed. 'Good man.'

'Glad you think so,' was the dry response. 'You don't think he's the kind who could have got his corpses confused, then?'

He was playing with me, but I didn't mind. It was generous of Rourke to cooperate with me at all. If he

31

wanted to throw a few rocks in the process, I was in no position to complain.

'I doubt it. Just routine. One last thing, John, and then I'll leave you to get on cleaning up the city. This man Lockhart. What did Gil Randall think of him?'

'Couldn't find a thing against him,' was the answer, but I felt he was being evasive.

'Nothing to put in, a report, you mean. Wasn't what I asked you. The question was, what did Gil think?'

Rourke closed the file, and laid it to one side.

'He didn't take to the man. It wasn't anything he could put his finger on. Just didn't like him. I think it was probably prejudice. You know Gil. He has a good healthy mind where the women are concerned. He wouldn't be able to take to a man that age, living with a woman so much older. A few years is one thing. A quarter of a century is something else besides. That's about what it was. You know Gil.'

I knew Gil, all right. Knew him well enough to have a great deal of respect for his judgement when it came to people.

'Well thanks, John, I'm obliged to you.'

When I reached the door, he said softly.

'Oh, just before you go, there was one little thing. If you happen to come across anything that might interest a tired old public servant, you'll be sure to let me in on it. Right?'

The words were warm and friendly. The eyes were cold.

'You bet,' I assured him. 'Thanks again.'

32

THREE

I put a call through to Prentiss and Prentiss. Mr Prentiss Junior would not be free at all that day. Mr Prentiss the Third however could give me ten minutes if I went along right away. After that, he had to appear in court, and there was no telling when his next free period might be. I got over there fast, reflecting that I was lucky to get such quick access. It was a relief to hear that 'Third' tag on the Prentiss name. Since John Rourke had confused me with that Junior business, I'd been trying to work out how Junior's son would be described. 'Minor' didn't sound exactly right on a grown man. But then, you don't come across all that many septuagenarians called Junior either. The Third, now. That was a nice solution.

The offices were not the dusty cramped quarters I half-expected. Instead, they were practically space-age. A twinkling aluminium globe was set in the floor of the reception area, reflecting directional lamps which hung from the walls and ceiling. It was more like a sci-fi movie set than a lawyer's waiting room. Not that there was anything fictional about the pneumatic blonde behind the gleaming metal desk. Her face was expressionless behind heavy pan make-up as I approached. Then somebody switched on her smile. It lasted one point five seconds, after which she waited.

'I was going to ask if Captain Kirk was around, but I

expect you've heard it before.'

'Not today,' she replied, in a tone as expressionless as the rest of her. 'Five times yesterday. The record day was last month. Fourteen times I was asked the same question. We're running a lottery on the total between now and Christmas. It's a dollar a ticket. Can I interest you?'

With some dames that could have been a provocative opening. With this one, it was an invitation to buy a lottery ticket.

'No thanks,' I replied. 'Lotteries are against the law. I'll mention it to Mr Prentiss the Third. I have an appointment, as of now. Name is Preston.'

She nodded. 'Yes, I know. Second door on the left.'

I walked over the shining floor, hoping we wouldn't run into a flock of meteorites. There was no grab-rail for me to hang onto. Who's designing our starships these days?

Mr Prentiss the Third was pushing forty, and fighting it. Thinning hair cut en brosse above a square face on which the side-burns were too long. Too. That was the key word. He was a too man. The shirt was too bright, the tie too wide. Expensive cloth was too tapered at the waist. His shoes were out of sight, but you knew they would be too, too.

'Good of you to see me Mr Prentiss,' I opened.

'Well, you said it was urgent,' he reminded. 'But I have a few minutes before I leave for the courts. What can I do for you, Mr Preston?'

Clearly, we were not going to waste much time on formalities, and that suited me.

'Your firm has the handling of the estate of a lady who died last week. A Mrs Honoria Lockhart.'

'Do we?' He wasn't being difficult, I could tell. This was a big outfit, and the late Honoria's affairs were obviously being dealt with by somebody else. 'What did you wish to know about it?'

'Damned if I know, to tell you the truth,' I confessed. 'The point is, I have been hired by a lady who may or may not be a beneficiary. There is just an outside possibility that some of Mrs Lockhart's effects may have a much greater value than is generally believed.'

I paused, to give him an opportunity to press me.

'I'd have to ask you to elaborate on that.'

He was interested now. This was the kind of stuff that put a spark of life into the law business. Valuable effects, eh?

'I can't be certain, you understand. There are many questions to be asked yet. Did you read that case a few weeks ago, where some old guy had left a lifetime collection of tin soldiers? He wasn't anybody much. A janitor at some block of flats. Outside of the collection, he was worth about two cents, less tax. The family were thinking of giving the soldiers to an orphanage, but somebody got wind of it. When the stuff finally went up for auction, it realised something over seventy thousand dollars. Do you recall it now?'

He smiled. 'Very clearly. So does the whole profession. The case is still going on, and it will be for months. Years, probably. Nothing divides a family like money, Mr Preston. Are you suggesting we may have something

35

of the same kind here?'

The prospect certainly seemed to appeal to him. I seemed to have struck the right note.

'It seems that Mrs Lockhart had collected a great number of old drawings. Not in the art gallery sense. These things come under the heading of calligraphy. Kind of stuff you see in very old bibles, and medieval books. There is some of it at the Spanish Museum, collected from the California monasteries. Very fine work.'

'I know the kind of thing you mean. I suppose it could be valuable, to a specialist collector. What point are you making?'

I took a deep breath, and mixed in a little extra sincerity.

'The point is this. Mrs Lockhart always promised my client that she could have one of the drawings as a keepsake. Only one, mark you, out of many dozens. The husband, Franklin Lockhart, has refused to let her have one.'

Mr Prentiss the Third was looking sadly wise.

'This is a very old story, I'm afraid. It's happening every day. Sometimes it's a silver teapot, or a discarded fur coat. Not always something valuable, either. Quite often a keepsake, as you say. Offhand, I would say that these verbal undertakings cause more trouble among the survivors than the terms of the will itself. If you have come here hoping that I can give you a legal ruling about this drawing, I'm going to have to disappoint you.'

I wagged my head sideways.

'Certainly not. I'm no lawyer, but I know better than that.'

'Well then?' He looked at his watch.

'The point is, Mr Prentiss, that Mr Lockhart has no interest in the drawings. My client tells me that he used to scoff at his wife's hobby. Waste of time and money, that kind of remark. So why should he refuse to part with one of them?'

Prentiss shrugged. 'Who can tell why people do things? Perhaps the man now has a great sentimental interest in them. Or perhaps he just doesn't like your client. I really don't see where all this is leading us.'

The heave-ho was looming close. I had to play the only card I had.

'You could be right, of course. But there is another possibility. We could have a tin soldier case here. Lockhart may have had an expert in to value the collection, and found he is sitting on a goldmine. Or a tin mine perhaps.'

His thin, watery smile was about what the gag deserved.

'Even so?'

'Supposing I'm right. Supposing Lockhart is only waiting his time, and intends to sell the collection after a suitable period? Wouldn't that constitute some kind of tax evasion? I mean, I'm in your hands here, Mr Prentiss. You'd have to guide me on that. But it does seem to a layman that the Bureau of Internal Revenue might be interested.'

'Could be, I suppose,' he began. Then 'in fact yes,

most certainly, now that I give it more thought.'

I rushed ahead, holding this slight advantage.

'Well then, if that were to happen, couldn't it be possible for the Revenue boys to feel annoyed with Prentiss and Prentiss for not having thought about it?'

'H'm.'

He leaned back. The urgency of his departure seemed to have lost its edge.

'It occurred to me,' I pressed on, 'that you would probably want to avoid any criticism of that kind. Indeed, that you might wish to do something positive to forestall it.'

There was a glint of amusement in his eyes now.

'Such as hiring a certain well-known and undoubtedly expensive private investigator to look into the matter on our behalf? Is that what you had in mind?'

I gave him my offended look.

'Certainly not,' I denied. 'There are ethics involved here. I couldn't take money from two different sources for the same investigation. I already have a client. What I'm trying to get across is that I shall be looking after your firm's interests, purely as a side benefit.'

'At no charge?'

'At no charge.'

He nodded, as though satisfied. But, bright shirt or no, he wasn't a lawyer for nothing.

'Most gratifying, Mr Preston. I can assure you, on the firm's behalf, that we appreciate your concern for our good name, and that we shall await developments with interest. However,' and he looked at me down the broad

38

nose, 'you didn't come in here just to tell me that. You want something. What is it? And I really do have to leave in the next two minutes.' He tapped at his watch.

'I'd like to have a sight of the will,' I replied flatly.

'May I ask why?'

'I'd like to know about the other beneficiaries, if there are any. As things stand, I believe the estate is very small, so no one is getting especially excited. A valuable collection could change all that.'

'Do you mean you would get in touch with these people, get some litigation started?'

'No,' I assured him. 'That isn't what I meant at all. I intend to go and talk to Franklin Lockhart. The more knowledgeable I sound about the terms of the will, the more the position I'll be in will be a sound one. In any case, the will is more or less public property by now. You're not giving away any deep secrets.'

'That's true.' A final glance at the watch, and he stood up. 'Very well. I'll have the file looked out, and someone will talk to you. It won't be me, I'm afraid. I have to go now. Let me say that I appreciate your attitude, so far as our interests are concerned. If anything in your line of work should cross my desk in the future, I shall not forget that we are in your debt.'

It seemed to be a time for a general standing up.

'Thank you Mr Prentiss. I appreciate the cooperation.'

We shook hands briefly.

'If you will just wait here,' he told me, 'someone will be along.'

He went out, and I waited here. By the time I had made an inventory of the comfortable furniture and the expensive fittings, the door was opening again. One look at the newcomer, and there I was repeating that standing up routine.

She was five three, nut-brown hair pulled tight behind the ears and tied in a loose pony tail. Dark horn-rims, the size of saucers, perched halfway down a strong nose, partly obscured the pale green of her eyes. Pretty, too, although the mouth was too large for perfection. As to the rest of her, she was doing her best to look businesslike. The high-throated, knee-length dress of thin gray wool was exactly what your modern executive lady ought to wear. Trouble was, the average modern executive lady didn't have to package the same contents as this one. On her it just looked sexy.

I tried to stand even straighter. The green eyes regarded me severely.

'Mr Preston? I am Hortense Mulligan.'

Hortense? Ah, well.

'How do, Miss Mulligan. Would that be the Lockhart file you're holding?'

'It would,' she confirmed.

Not quite daring to occupy the distinguished seat which belonged properly to Mr Prentiss the Third, she shifted another chair behind the desk, and perched herself to one side. This manoeuvre took her legs out of view, but there was plenty left to feast on. Opening the folder, she laid it flat in front of her. She was waiting for something, and for a moment I wasn't sure what. Then it

40

dawned on me that I was still standing there, and this was a sitting situation. I made myself as tall as I could in the chair.

'I am the attorney dealing with the Lockhart estate,' she informed me crisply. 'Mr Prentiss has instructed me to give you any information you require. How can I help you?'

Hell of a question to put to a simple male. A quick run out to Catalina would help, but a week down in Acapulco would be better. This probably was not the kind of help she had immediately in mind, but I couldn't help feeling the subject might be introduced at some future time.

To open with, I stuck to the line I'd opened with her boss. He would probably ask her to report, when he got back.

'Beneficiaries,' I began. 'Could you tell me the other names, please? Outside of Mr Lockhart, that is.'

'Very quickly,' she replied. 'There are none.'

It was not a very good beginning.

'None at all?' I said feebly.

She didn't exactly sigh, but her tone did.

'That was the impression I was attempting to convey.'

'Oh. So Mr Lockhart gets everything?'

'That would seem to follow,' she confirmed, sweetly.

If I was trying to make a good impression on Hortense Mulligan, I wasn't doing too well up to that point.

'Could you tell me the net value?'

'Eleven hundred and forty-three dollars, twenty-six cents,' she announced. 'Plus an insurance policy.'

41

She turned over some pages.

Insurance policy. This would be the big one. This would be where the fifty thousand came in, the hundred thousand. I waited anxiously.

'Yes, here it is. The policy is for three thousand dollars.'

Hortense folded her hands on the desk top, and waited for the next question. I decided to play innocent.

'I don't understand this at all,' I muttered. 'I would have thought the house alone would be worth forty thousand or more.'

'Quite possibly,' she agreed. 'But the house did not belong to Mrs Lockhart. It is the property of her sister, Miss Rowena Parker.'

Innocence pays off sometimes. Like now. So the wealthy sister, far from being the stand-offish character described by Mrs Fyffe, had in fact given Honoria a roof. And a comfortable one, too.

'Thank you. I hadn't realised that. There was something else, too. As I understand it, Mrs Lockhart had an income from her father's estate. Do you have any information as to what became of that income on her death?'

She did her best to introduce puzzled furrows on her forehead, but the smooth skin resisted.

'Father's estate? I have no record of any such income. Nothing at all. So far as I am aware, Mrs Lockhart's sole source of support was a regular small monthly allowance made, again, by her sister. Are you sure of your facts, Mr Preston?'

'No,' I admitted. 'No, I'm not. It seems quite possible that I have been misled. I'm sure your facts will be the right one. Miss Parker seems to be a most generous lady. Do you know her at all?'

She seemed to withdraw even further behind the giant spectacles.

'I met her once, here in the office,' she informed me. 'She seemed a most charming woman.'

'Could you tell me any more about her?' I asked casually.

A little more of the ice-floe poked its head above the surface.

'I could not,' she said primly. 'And even if I could, I wouldn't. I am instructed to help you over the Lockhart estate, not to discuss the firm's clients.'

'Ah. Then Miss Parker is a client.'

Realising that she'd let something slip, she flushed.

'Not of mine. If you wish to talk to someone about the lady, you would have to make an appointment with Mr Prentiss Junior.'

It was time to play the innocent again.

'Junior,' I echoed. 'You mean Mr Prentiss has a son here? He hardly looks old enough.'

At last I had struck a welcome note. The lady lawyer almost grinned.

'It would seem to be your day for being misled, Mr Preston. The youthful image presented by Mr Prentiss the Third tends to belie his age. He may think he is twenty-five, but he isn't.' Evidently the Third was not highly placed among Hortense's favorite people. 'But

43

that's another matter. Mr Prentiss Junior is in fact the senior partner. He is the Third's father.'

I looked like a man trying desperately to understand, so she went on to explain once more the story I'd already heard. At the end, I smiled.

'Complicated, isn't it? Junior being the head man, and everything. From what you say, I gather the boss handles Miss Parker's affairs personally. That must mean he's still active.'

She considered for a moment, and I guessed she was trying to decide whether to tell me to mind my own business again. The decision went in my favor this time.

'Mr Prentiss Junior is letting go of the reins gradually,' she explained. 'But with the more elderly clients he deals with things himself. He takes the view, and I'm sure he's right, that older people feel more sympatico with someone in their own age bracket. They like to see a few gray hairs, and exchange views about how much better things used to be. It gives them confidence in the firm, and confidence is everything in the law business.'

'That makes sense,' I agreed. 'You're going to have to wait quite a while before any of those people get steered in your direction. About fifty years, I would guess.'

The amused twinkle in the green eyes belonged to the woman, not the lawyer.

'You're very kind, but forty would be nearer the mark. I've already been practising for three years.'

That's the trouble with the world today, there's no communication. Here was this item, working almost under my nose for the past three years, and I'd never even laid eyes on her until that very day.

'Look, I may need some more help on this case. I don't work office hours, so it could be any time. If something should crop up, is there a number where I could reach you?'

She lowered her eyes.

'I have a rule,' she explained. 'I never discuss the firm's business outside office hours. That is my private time.'

'Better yet,' I persisted. 'I'd like to discuss your private time.'

Picking up the file, she got to her feet.

'Was there anything else about the Lockhart estate?'

She was getting rid of me, but I detected a lack of emphasis.

'Thank you, no. I'm most grateful for the cooperation.'

We walked to the door, and I opened it for her.

'Thank you.' She turned, and looked up at me. 'There's a telephone on my desk, of course. If it rings, I have to answer it.'

I nodded my understanding.

'I have a feeling that it will.'

Outside, the world seemed a more cheerful, go-ahead sort of place. There seemed to be a feeling of promise in the air, well, half-promise. Hortense Mulligan had brought a whole new dimension to things.

FOUR

There are a lot of people in this world who like to think they know something about everything. In fact, they don't need a lot of encouragement to give you the impression they know everything about anything. I spent a few fruitless years trying to get in on that scene, but after I'd been wrong the first million times, I tried a new approach, and it worked. These days, I know nothing about anything. What I do, to compensate for these vast gaps in my knowledge, is to be sure I know someone who does know. It works on all levels. It gives pleasure to my sources, for one thing. Nobody can resist an opportunity to show off his knowledge. It not only makes him feel good, it puts him into the role of benefactor, which isn't easy to resist. It also takes a lot of the hassle out of my own existence. I don't have to bother with cramming my mind with all kinds of extraneous information, in the hope that it may be useful some day. The only information I have to store is the names and locations of people to whom I can refer, on a huge variety of subjects. They are usually glad to be called on, and nobody ever refuses. Who can refuse an open invitation to show off his feathers?

I suppose I'm what you might call a professional ignoramus, and if you think that's bad at first glance, chew on it for a while. Consider the trouble-free existence it brings. It's like having all human knowledge stored on my private computer, with a significant difference. All my terminals are human beings, and that beats any machine that's been produced so far.

Take this calligraphy thing, for example. All I knew about calligraphy was that it was not the name of a Roman emperor, but had something to do with old writing. Or so I thought. I didn't have to bother myself any further than that. All I had to do was pick up a telephone and push a few buttons. My art terminal is a man named Josh Holland.

'New Holland Gallery, good afternoon.'

I keep meaning to ask Josh about his receptionist. She has this voice like warm cream being strained through velvet. Even over the telephone, a man has to pull in his waistline.

'And good afternoon to you,' I purred. 'Will you put me through to Mr Holland, please. Tell him my name is Preston. Mark Preston.'

'I'll see whether Mr Holland is available.'

I spent the waiting time wondering whether Mr Holland's receptionist might be available. Two clickings, and he was on the line.

'Preston? Zattu? How're you?'

I was fine, and how was he, and he was fine, and how were things, and things were fine too. We were off, you might say, to a fine start.

'Listen Josh, how are you fixed on calligraphy?'

'Calligraphy?' he repeated. 'Why, what are you up to?'

'Just routine,' I assured him. 'There's a thing I'm working on, and one of the people dabbles in it. I'd like to know something about it, so I don't get fooled too easily.'

'Dabbles in it?' he queried. 'You wouldn't fool a simple old picture-dealer, now would you? Are you sure some old Indian hasn't dug up a bucketful of medieval manuscripts? Little shopping lists the monks left lying around? It's happened before.'

Josh Holland, in common with all his fraternity, never loses faith that the big one is going to land in his lap one day.

'Cross my heart, Josh,' I assured him. 'This is strictly an amateur. Well, can you help me with it?'

'Not really,' he told me. 'I see very little of that kind of thing. Doesn't hit the market very often. You need a scholar.'

'Do you know one?'

'Don't be offensive,' he said huffily. 'Certainly I know one. Matter of fact, you're in luck. There are only about a dozen people in the whole country I could recommend. One of them is right here. Out at Berkeley, in fact. Professor Carl d'Agostini. Top man on illuminations.'

We seemed to be getting off the point.

'Illuminations? Listen, I don't need a lighting engineer,' I protested.

There was a prolonged sigh at the other end.

'You know, Preston, I sometimes wonder how such an ignorant man can get across the street unaided. I'm not talking about lighting. The whole subject comes under

48

the heading of illuminations. Do me a favor. If you're going to use my name as a reference, try not to let the professor know you as well as I do. I have to think of my reputation.'

Although he couldn't see me, I grinned anyway.

'd'Agostini? Got it. Thanks a lot, Josh.'

'Listen, if it turns out you find yourself stuck with something valuable, you'll know where to bring it to market, right?'

'You got it,' I told him, 'but don't wait up. It's my guess this stuff is trash.'

Holland sounded unimpressed when he replied.

'Your guess? Yes, well I don't consider that too final. You're the kind of character who would use a Van Gogh to cover a damp patch on the wall.'

'I love you too,' I assured him. 'Oh, by the way Josh, about your receptionist—'

'No,' he cut in. 'Just no. You wouldn't like her anyway. She's eighty-three years old, and wears a wig. My wife's grandmother, as a matter of fact.'

The receptionist, evidently, was already spoken for.

'Oh. Well, she does sound a little young for me. Thanks for the help. I'll let you know how it comes out.'

We broke off, and I looked up the number of the university. It took them quite a while to track down the professor, who didn't appear to receive many telephone calls. He sounded pleasant enough, when we finally made contact, and agreed to see me after his next class. That gave me one hour to make the trip. I would need every minute of it, with afternoon traffic the way it was.

49

Luckily for me, I knew my way around that vast campus, and made it to the meeting spot with a whole minute in hand. There was no problem about how to while away the time, as I waited for the professor to show. The place is alive with females, strolling hither and yon, and a mere male soon finds himself becoming confused about where to look next. Not every male, I realised. There was a short, rotund little character, about sixty years old, walking along beside a bouncing fluffball about forty years his junior, and they were deep in conversation. Disgusting, I reflected. The kid ought to know better, even if he didn't. Then, when they were a few yards away, she said, loud enough for me to hear

'Till Thursday, then. And I won't be late.'

The little guy nodded and beamed. Then he came up to me.

'Mr Preston? I'm Carl d'Agostini.'

We shook hands.

'Good of you to see me, professor.'

'How could I refuse?' he chuckled. 'Most of the world doesn't even know I'm alive. Even around here, people sometimes wonder who I am and what I do. To have someone come especially all the way from Monkton City is an intriguing event. What can I do for you? No, don't tell me yet. Let's go to my house and have a glass of tea. Very refreshing at this time of day.'

'Thank you. That would be fine. Will I need the car?'

'No. It's only a five-minute walk.'

I fell into step beside him.

'Do you have another class today?' I asked, by way of

50

conversation.

He turned towards me, with a look of amusement.

'Not today. Nor tomorrow. I'm free now until Thursday. Two classes per week, and this is a busy year.'

There was obviously some meaning there, but it was lost on me.

'You mean it's more than usual?'

'Let me explain. My subject is something of a rarity. You might call it almost esoteric. Not many young people are interested. It's a far cry from computers. Last year, I had no students at all. This year, one. You probably saw me talking to her just now.'

So the fluffball was his class. It made me feel better disposed towards him. Plus a little guilty for jumping to conclusions.

'Seemed like a bright little thing.'

'Bright enough,' he confirmed. 'An archaeology major really, but she's taking me as an extra. That's the house over there.'

It was the inevitable little white-frame, with a few colored shrubs dotted around in front. The door wasn't even locked. Inside, the expected colonial furniture seemed thoroughly at home,

'Sit down, Mr Preston, while I make the tea. Do you take lemon in it?'

'Please.'

I pulled out my Old Favorites, looking around for an ashtray. There wasn't one, so I put the pack reluctantly back in my pocket. On the walls, a few photographs claimed my attention. There was one of the professor,

51

receiving an award at the Smithsonian Institute in Washington. Another showed his shaking hands with an important-looking man, outside a place called the Biblioteca Laurenziana in Florence, Italy. I was staring at the pictures when he came back into the room, carrying two steaming glasses.

'I see you are looking at the photographs. Mine is a narrow field, Mr Preston. There are only a few hundred of us in the entire world. We like to keep in touch, give each other prizes. It is our way of reminding each other that we really do exist.'

I grinned, and took the glass from him. It smelled good.

'Seems to take you around quite a bit,' I offered.

He nodded, sitting down where we could look at each other.

'I spend each summer in one of the great museums. There is always so much to learn, so much I haven't seen. The sad thing is, I shall only have scratched the surface, having spent my entire life at it. And you, what do you do, Mr Preston?'

I set the tea down on a narrow glass table.

'I'm a private investigator,' I told him. 'When I tell that to people, I also like to make it plain that I don't do divorce work. I don't spend my life taking pictures through hotel windows. There's plenty of other work to be had.'

'It must be very exciting,' he suggested.

'Not often,' I denied. 'Mostly it's just plodding around, asking a lot of questions, being told a lot of lies.

Sometimes I get lucky, and something a little out of the ordinary crops up. This is one of those times.'

'Ah,' he smiled. 'We come to the denouement. That is the word, isn't it?'

The professor was enjoying himself. A man didn't have to be brilliant detective to realise that he led a lonely existence.

'A lady died recently, in Monkton,' I began. 'She wasn't a rich woman, by any stretch of the imagination. The only interesting thing about her was this interest in calligraphy. At least, that's the word I was given. Josh Holland said I probably meant illuminations. I wouldn't know.'

He removed the slice of lemon from his glass and squeezed the juice carefully into his tea. Then he wiped his fingers on a large handkerchief.

'This is most interesting,' he said slowly. 'The subject does not attract a great deal of attention.'

'That's what I thought,' I agreed. 'It seems this lady spent a lot of her time doing this work. She left behind, and this is only hearsay you understand, hundreds of drawings. Now, it happens sometimes in the art world that an unknown painter dies, and suddenly his work becomes valuable. I was wondering—'

'You were wondering whether something of the kind might have happened here,' he finished. 'Well, I hate to disappoint you, Mr Preston, but the answer is no. I'll explain that in more detail in a moment. I am intrigued by this lady. Would you be permitted to tell me her name?'

I couldn't see the relevance, but there was no harm in the request.

'Certainly,' I said. 'She was a Mrs Lockhart. Honoria Lockhart.'

He tapped smartly at his knee.

'Hah. I was hoping it might be. I have corresponded with this lady.'

My look of surprise was not assumed.

'Well, I must say this is a terrific coincidence.'

'Not really,' he contradicted. 'Not when you think about it. If you suddenly wanted to take up a subject, where would you go for advice? You would obviously go to someone who knew something about it. If you wanted to learn to drive, for example, you would go to a driving instructor. There are many of them, of course. Stamp collecting, rare butterflies. There are people you can approach about these things, and they will be glad to help you. But if you want to become involved with calligraphy, or, as our friend Holland correctly says, "illumination", you have to come to me. It's a little like Tigger in the Pooh stories. I, Mr Preston, am the only one. That isn't conceit, you understand. Merely a statement of fact.'

It was true, too. Whatever else he might be, there was no evidence of conceit about the professor.

'Yes, I can see that. But it's still very fortunate for me. Could you tell me more about your correspondence with Mrs Lockhart?'

'Certainly. Let me see, it would be about five years ago, when she first wrote to me. That would be right, I think. She said she had become interested in the subject, and could I advise her on how to go about it. Naturally, I was delighted to do what I could. I told her which books to read, what materials to buy, that kind of thing. I suppose we wrote to each other two or three times altogether. I haven't heard from her in a long time. And now, the poor lady is dead. I'm sorry to hear it. I would have liked to see some of her work. I suppose that wouldn't be possible?'

He sounded as though his interest was real enough, and I thought I knew the reason. A man with so few students would naturally want to know about their progress. Even someone who was only a correspondent would have a place in the thoughts of this lonely man. But there was something else which intrigued me more.

'I wouldn't know, professor,' I admitted. 'The husband is reputed to be a difficult man. I'm due to see him very soon, and there's no harm in my telling him about your interest. I'll let you know what he says.'

'Oh, would you really? I'd certainly appreciate it.'

'No trouble at all,' I assured him. 'Tell me though, how come you recognise her name? Five years ago, she wasn't married. The name was Parker, then. She only became Lockhart a little over a year ago.'

I didn't like to quiz the man, but I was hoping it would turn out he'd had a letter from her more recently than his memory supposed.

'Ah,' and his face lit up. 'This is like the final scene in one of those courtroom dramas, isn't it?' He deepened his voice, and affected a dramatic tone. 'Unfortunately for you, professor, you made one small slip in your testimony. A slip which will lead you to the condemned cell. Mrs Lockhart could not have written to you five years ago, because Mrs Lockhart did not exist then. It was you who poisoned the cat, and sank the Titanic.'

He was having a whale of a time, and I couldn't help enjoying it with him.

'Well, did you? Sink the Titanic?'

'No, I did not, and I can prove it. She went down ten years before I was born.'

That seemed to get him off the Titanic charge.

'What about Mrs Lockhart/Parker?'

'Even more prosaic, I regret. I had a printed card from the lady. You know, the usual formal thing. She didn't even bother to put a personal note on it. I must have been on some business list. Along with the telephone company and the rest. Your next question should be, how did I remember the name so easily? The answer is, cataloguing is an essential part of my work. I have to have a memory like a filing system.'

I nodded, seeing the sense of that.

'Thank you. Tell me, though, why were you so definite that her work couldn't have any value?'

'Ah yes. I promised to explain that, didn't I? You see, in one way, we are speaking of a dead art. In former time, the illustrators of manuscripts did their work more or less to make the finished product more attractive to the eye, more interesting. They almost seemed to compete with each other in the amount of information they could cram into a small space. The art has been handed down to us from a date no one can ascertain. The nature of the work, you see, the materials used, make it very susceptible to the ravages of time.'

The professor's tone began to take on a declamatory element. If I didn't stop him soon, I would be getting the full platform lecture.

'Then what would Mrs Lockhart have been doing?' I wanted to know. 'I mean, if there's no demand for original work, presumably all people can do is to copy?'

It was the first time his facial expression had been anything other than benevolent.

'Copy?' he echoed. 'I can't say that I'm altogether impressed with your choice of words, Mr Preston. Emulate, perhaps. Yes, emulate. Many people have tried, some with a fair measure of success. It's a formidable task, believe me. The amount of information the ancients could cram into a square inch, even sometimes into a single letter, was amazing. That is the fascination of my field, you see. I am, in my way, a detective like yourself. The detail in these illuminations tells us more about the daily lives of the times than many an antique manuscript. There are people who tend to discuss the illuminators as very minor artists, and that is a whole subject by itself. But no one can deny the brilliance of their craftsmanship, nor ignore the value of the information they give us. Take the iconography of the Islamic period, for instance—'

The lecture was on again. I had a choice. I could either be resigned, or rude. Well, what the hell? I had asked the man to help me, and he was doing his best. Let him talk.

He talked.

'—and it is particularly sad to be aware that there was actually a painted portrait of no less a scholar than Virgil himself, now lost. In one way, we are fortunate to know of its very existence, since it is referred to specifically in Martial's Epigrams, but at the same time, it is very tantalising to be aware of our loss.'

It was pleasantly warm in the room, and the lemon tea had a refreshing tang. d'Agostini flowed on, not quietly like that guy Don, but with an impassioned sincerity which compelled me to listen. The minutes ticked away.

'At the Bibliotheque Nationale in Paris, there is one Byzantine plate of particular value in this connection—'

There was more, lots more. I was reduced to clutching at the now-cooling tea-glass, and staring at the lecturer in a state of near-mesmerism. I think something must have communicated itself to him, because he broke off suddenly.

'However, you mustn't get me started, Mr Preston.'

Started. He actually said started.

'Not a bit,' I denied, standing up, before he changed his mind. 'It has all been most interesting, and I'm very grateful for your time. One thing, though. Why should Mrs Lockhart have used the term calligraphy for this work? You've hardly mentioned the word.'

'Ah yes,' he shrugged. 'It's not an uncommon assumption in the world at large. Calligraphy itself is a much narrower field. It is simply the art of lettering. What the ancients did was to foresee the use which could be made of the spaces within the letters. They began to inscribe pictures into those spaces within the letters, and this led to the whole business of illuminations proper. The calligrapher simply made the letters themselves more flowery, more ornate. Very fine work it is, too. Don't let me leave you with the impression that I am dismissing them as of no importance. What I am saying is, their work is there to be admired for itself. The illuminators are the people who speak to us through their work.'

'But Mrs Lockhart was working on both?'

'As to that, I couldn't say without seeing what she actually did. But certainly, after her initial approach to me, she became interested in what I had to tell her about illuminations. Some of the materials she wanted would have been more appropriate to that work than to straight-forward lettering. Don't forget you promised to ask whether I could see some of it.'

'I won't forget.'

He walked me outside. It was a peaceful sight out there, and I reflected on the difference in our life-styles. Here, there were flowers and birds. When I'd gone, the professor would disappear back into his comfortable house, and his comfortable secret world of past heroes and triumphs. Where I was going, there was concrete, steel and plastic. No heroes, and not many triumphs. Just worried people, in grubby streets. The illuminators had been replaced by the instant camera. That was a heartening thought. At least, when a wandering space-visitor dropped in on Earth, five or six thousand years ahead, he would find plenty of pictorial evidence of what we had looked like. He would be able to see for himself

the faces of the people who finally blew up the planet.
It's nice to know one's place in antiquity is assured.

When I drove away, I was thoughtful.

FIVE

At last I was on my way to talk with Franklin Lockhart. When you boiled it right down, he was the only person who mattered in this investigation. He was the man my client wanted locked up, and all the chasing around I'd been doing so far came under the heading of background filling. The next hour or so ought to tell me whether or not I was wasting Mrs Fyffe's time. I wasn't too hopeful. Sheila Fyffe's information had proved to be less than twenty two carat on some matters of basic fact. Her late friend had not owned the house, for one thing. The private income she received had not come from any estate of her father's. In both cases, the sister, Rowena, was cast as the good fairy, and that gave the lie to another part of the Fyffe report. If the sister was as stand-offish as was claimed, she had a funny way of showing it. She had provided Honoria with a good home, and enough money to keep it running. That didn't sound to me like the behavior of an estranged relative. On the contrary, it showed a degree of generosity un- usual in families. There were two possible explanations for Sheila Fyffe's story. She could have been jealous of Rowena Parker. Jealous of her money, for one thing, and equally jealous of the influential part she played in Honoria's life. These middle-aged ladies can get very touchy about their friendships.

Or, it may not have been that way at all. The late Honoria could have been responsible. She could have told Mrs Fyffe a pack of lies about her personal circumstances. People can be very resentful towards their benefactors. It's just one of those human quirks. Maybe Honoria had been eaten up with envy of her better-placed sister, and wasn't going to let her have any credit for her generosity.

As I chewed over this last possibility, I realised quite suddenly that I may have come up with a motive for murder.

Supposing I was right. Supposing Honoria had told Sheila Fyffe a pack of lies about the house, and her source of income? Wasn't it possible that she had fed Franklin Lockhart the same yarn? It would have been understandable if she had. A woman in her position, setting out to get a man twenty-five years her junior, would want to make the setting as attractive as she could. She would want him to be aware that she wasn't going to impose any financial burden. Quite the reverse, in fact. She was in a position to offer him a comfortable home, and an income to go with it. If she had already sold her friend Sheila a bill of goods about those arrangements, was it stretching the imagination too far to think she may have told Lockhart the same story?

The answer was no. And the motive for murder was right there.

Until then, I'd been falling into the same trap as everybody else. I'd only been looking at the facts. Just

62

like Rourke. There was no profit to be made from Honoria Lockhart's death, and all the facts proved it. Ergo, no murder. But this new line of thinking could change that picture drastically. We were all dealing with facts. Incontestable, undeniable fact. What we did not know, and had no way of knowing, was whether those facts had been available to Franklin Lockhart. Because, if they hadn't, he could have been under the impression that he would inherit the house, and maybe some capitalisation of the income along with it. In other words, he could have murdered Honoria, only to find it was for nothing.

I couldn't drive sensibly in the busy traffic while this new concept was dominating my attention. Pulling into the side, I switched off the engine, and dug out my Old Favorites. It was all supposition, of course. It didn't lead anywhere. Even if it were true, no one could ever prove it. And yet, the more I thought about it, the more I liked it. If it had been that way, then Franklin Lockhart had to be the most disappointed man in town. To go to the length of murdering someone, only to find that the pot of gold had been swiped, would have a damaging effect on a person's faith. I spent another ten minutes in the car. Just sitting there, adjusting my thoughts, and deciding on how best to approach the bereaved and grieving widower.

Then I moved back into traffic, and headed for Montenero Drive.

There had been nothing to take me out that way for a year or two. Nothing had changed. Everything was just as neat, just as orderly, just as predictable. Things would never change around there, not perceptibly. The carefully-spaced trees would get taller and thicker, but otherwise everything would be the same. It's reassuring to feel that some things will last. Most of the properties were built in what we now call ranch-style, although what the old-time cowpokes would have said to that is not recorded. Number Twenty-One was flanked by Nineteen and Twenty-Three. The door of the up-over garage was painted a brilliant green, in contrast with, respectively, sky-blue and lethal red. There were one or two sprinklers in action on the pool-table lawns, and the sun formed small rainbows above the dancing spray. Even the rainbows seemed to fall symmetrically within the plot boundaries. There was to be no disorder here, evidently, not even from natural causes.

Natural causes. That brought me right back to the purpose of my visit. A mixture of alcohol and drugs, however induced, does not produce death by natural causes. I pulled in outside number twenty-one, and climbed out of the car, closing the door quietly. Then I walked up the little path to the front door, where a black floral tribute dangled grimly. The buzzer caused a mellow gong-like sound within the house. Nothing happened. After about a minute, I tried again, without result. A peek into the side window of the garage told me there was an ageing Ford at home. That ought to mean there was a human being to go with it. This was no area for a constitutional walk.

Maybe Lockhart was at the back of the house, and

hadn't heard the gong. He could be listening to music or something, using headphones. These days, more doors go unanswered that way than people realise. I walked around the side of the house, peeking in at windows. The place looked tidy enough to suggest that the new widower was not a slob, whatever else he might be. At the rear, a small patio was decked out with a table and a few brightly-colored chairs. On the table stood a one-and-a-half pints bottle containing about one and a half inches of rum. Beside the bottle was a glass, lying on its side. Next to the glass was a man's head, ditto. The rest of the man was sprawled into one of the canvas chairs. Mr Lockhart was not listening to music today.

For a moment I thought he could be dead. Then there was a great sigh from somewhere inside him, and an exhalation of stale booze hung sourly in the air.

'Mr Lockhart?'

Nothing. I put a hand gently on his shoulder.

'Wake up, feller.'

Still nothing. I gave the shoulder a good shove.

'Lockhart, come to.'

As a candidate for this week's Genial Host, I had a scratch entry on my hands. Great. Behind me, a pair of french doors were propped open. After a last look at the proud owner, I went softly inside the house.

My initial impression was confirmed. There had been no woman's hand in there for a week, and yet everything was in its proper place. It was not the orderliness of a man doing his best. It was precise, almost scientific. A little too neat here, too square there. More like a display room in a store than a house someone really lived in. It was somehow familiar, and then I had it. Franklin Lockhart either had some military service in his background, or he'd spent a period in stir. Those were the only places I could think of, where the quarters are always ready for inspection. What I wanted to inspect were Honoria Lockhart's drawings, if I could find any. Also, any private papers I could get a sight of, that might tell me something about the Lockhart household, dead or alive. There was a small colonial bureau in one corner of the room. It wasn't locked, and after a quick peek over my shoulder at the motionless Franklin, I rummaged around inside. There seemed to be nothing of any interest at all. A handful of receipted bills, one or two more, yet to be paid, but too small to be significant. Probably, anything of importance would be in Lockhart's pockets, and I didn't know whether he was out cold enough for me to risk going through them.

Disappointed, I went through into the bedroom. Here was the same neatness, even the bed itself being properly made up. Out of habit I poked around underneath, and found two square flat boxes, which I pulled out. Lifting the lid of the first one, I realised I'd struck oil. There was a painting inside, not very big, but beautifully executed. There were men with beards and saintly expressions, one of them astride a mule. They wore ankle length white robes and thonged leather slippers. A man didn't have to be a teaching professor to know a religious painting when he saw one. The box was full of similar paintings and drawings, and when I opened the second

66

box, I found more of them. Despite what d'Agostini had said, I found it hard to accept that the collection was valueless. Looking at the workmanship, and thinking of the thousands of painstaking hours which must have gone into those end products, I felt that they didn't belong in a couple of boxes underneath a bed. It was a denial of Honoria Lockhart's existence. It was like something in a book I once read. If someone was judged to have offended against the system, then all references to him were deleted from the state records. With one computer entry, the guy not only ceased to exist, he never had existed, and the lack of record proved it. Well, we hadn't yet reached that stage, but those cardboard boxes represented the same kind of oblivion. Shoved out of sight, as a temporary measure. And then what? Tied up with string and stuck in an attic? Or worse. Simply fed into an incinerator, as worthless junk? The fact remained, that it really wasn't any of my business. I just felt that, living in a disposable society, we at least ought to try to keep a few things of our own producing. If these drawings had been five hundred years old, someone would have snapped them up fast enough. They would not have wound up under any bed. On impulse, I selected one of the pictures, and took it out. Then I put the rest back where I found them.

The telephone rang in the room behind me.

I went quickly out, and looked at the sprawled Lockhart. He showed no signs of hearing the muted ringing. I picked up the chocolate-colored plastic and put it to my ear.

'M'm?' I muttered.

There was a woman at the other end, and her voice was anxious.

'Joe?'

'M'm,' I confirmed.

'Have you got a cold or something?' she queried.

'Uh, uh,' I denied, guffly.

There was a slight pause, then she said.

'You've been drinking. Don't bother to deny it. I can hear it in your voice. I can't talk to you while you're half asleep. I'm coming over there.'

I put down the receiver, and considered. She could have got a wrong number, but I doubted it. I wondered how she managed to get the name Joe out of Franklin Lockhart. Anyway, all speculation would have to be put to one side for the moment. The lady was on her way, and I didn't want to be found in the house. Lockhart was in no condition to remember whether he'd answered the telephone or not. She wouldn't believe anything he said anyway, not once she saw the state he was in.

Picking up my picture, I started to leave by the same way that I'd come. Then I had a thought. Crossing to the table, I used a handkerchief to pick up the glass Lockhart had been drinking from. He'd never notice, and the woman would never question its absence. It would be easy to assume he'd been drinking straight from the bottle. I walked quickly back to the car, and put my prizes on the rear seat. Then I drove a hundred yards up the street, parking outside a little church, and settled down to watch number twenty-one. It wasn't one of those long stake-outs, mercifully. I hadn't been there more than fifteen minutes when a small white open two-seater came zipping past me, and screeched to a halt outside the Lockhart place. A woman jumped out, without opening the door, and walked quickly around the side. I gave her a couple of minutes start. Long enough to find the unconscious tenant, and to set about waking him up. Then, I drove slowly back to the house, making a great play of staring at the numbers again, in case she should be looking through a window. When I reached twenty-one, I wrote down the license number of the sports car, keeping my hand out of view. Then I climbed out, looking expectantly around like a man confirming he's found the right place. I walked once again up the front path, and leaned on the bell push. For a while there was no response. Then, a quick clack-clacking of high heels from inside, and the door was opened. She was thirty years old, with glossy black hair, swept up into a kind of topknot. The face was lively, with strong, almost hawk-like contours, dominated by a prominent nose beneath olive eyes. The eyes held me as they raked me over from top to toe, like a predator getting ready to dive. The rich tan of her skin was accentuated by the startling whiteness of the button-fronted shirt, tucked into red ski-pants. Lockhart had to be some kind of fool, I decided. If this one ever knocked on my door, I'd make damn sure I wasn't unconscious.

'Yes?'

'Is Mr Lockhart home?' I queried.

She hesitated. 'Who are you?'

'My name is Preston.'

I didn't offer anything else, curious to see how she would handle me.

'What do you want, Mr Preston?'

She was neither hostile nor friendly. Indifferent, almost.

'We just went through that,' I hedged. 'I want to see Mr Lockhart.'

That produced a little more reaction. A certain stubborness came into her face.

'He isn't feeling too well at the moment. There's been a bereavement here, you see.' She flicked a thumb towards the wreath. 'Perhaps I could help.'

'It's about the bereavement that I'm here,' I returned smoothly. 'Are you a member of the family, please?'

She hesitated, but not for long.

'A friend. I was a close friend of Mrs Lockhart's.'

I'll bet. I looked thoughtful, as if considering this new information.

'Friend? Well, I don't know. They didn't mention any friend.'

'They?' she came back quickly. 'Who are they?'

I looked surprised. 'Why, the lawyers. Prentiss and Prentiss. The firm who are dealing with Mrs Lockhart's estate. Mr Lockhart knows all about it. I spoke to him on the telephone less than an hour ago.'

'On the telephone?'

She bit her lip, anxious now. I was gambling on Lockhart's being unable to remember too well, when he pulled out of his drunk. The story would ring true to the woman. Hadn't she just had an unsatisfactory telephone conversation of her own with the same man? Besides which, the mention of the lawyers had given her something to think about.

'Why yes,' I declared, wide-eyed. 'Didn't he mention it to you?'

The dark head moved from side to side.

'No. I only just got here. As I say, he's not at all well. Perhaps if you came back later—?'

'I will,' I agreed. 'If Mr Lockhart says so. He would have to know that I must charge for two visits, if I do that. My time is pretty expensive, you see.'

She put a hand to the side of her head. The fingers were long and tapered, with no lacquer. The word 'expensive' had put her off her stride.

'Well, I don't know,' she hesitated.

'I really think you should ask him.' I persisted. 'Believe me, I know the fuss some people make when they get a bill. Seen it before, many times.'

Since it was obvious I had no intention of leaving, she made up her mind.

'Wait here a minute. I'll tell him what you said.'

She didn't even think to put the door on the latch, so she must have believed my honest face. I watched her stride back into the rear of the house, and it made nice watching. She walked like a dancer, or some kind of athlete, with strong confident movements that were graceful at the same time. Like I say, nice. There were voices next. Well, more accurately, there were two lots of human sounds. One was a voice, the woman's. The other was a series of grunts, oohs and aahs, from the stirring Lockhart. Then there was a movement, more voices and grunting, followed by the decisive click of a closing door.

She came back to me, smiling brightly.

'Mr Lockhart has asked me to speak for him. He really isn't up to it. Won't you come in, Mr Preston?'

I went through, and she led me into the orderly living room I'd already inspected. There was no one zonked out on the patio table, and the bedroom door was shut. Franklin had been pushed off to bed.

'This is a little irregular,' I opened hesitantly. 'I don't even know your name.'

'Of course,' she agreed. 'I'm Juliet Freeman. Now, if you'll just tell me what this is all about?'

I nodded without enthusiasm, still a man being convinced against his better judgement.

'Well, I guess, it's all right. You being such a friend of the deceased and everything.'

'We were very close,' she informed me gravely. 'In some ways Honoria took the place of the mother I never knew.'

That was a good line, I had to admit. It explained away the thirty years age gap, and put her in category one for sympathy, all in a few words. Not that she looked at me to be in much need of mothering.

'Then you will understand why it is important that something be done about the illuminations.'

'Illuminations?' she repeated, clearly puzzled.

Evidently her mother hadn't told her much about her

big hobby.

'The paintings, the drawings,' I explained patiently. 'You must know all about those?'

'Oh, yes. Yes, of course. Naturally. I just hadn't heard that word before. Well, what about them?'

She was all bright-eyed attention, and anxious to cooperate.

'Professor d'Agostini is anxious to see the collection,' I told her. 'Mrs Lockhart had been promising to have him over to the house, and of course he was very upset by her death.'

If she'd been treading water, before, she was floundering now.

'Professor d'Agostini? I don't think I know him.'

I permitted myself to look puzzled at that.

'The professor is a faculty member over at Berkeley. He and Mrs Lockhart were in close touch over her work. Are you saying she never mentioned him?'

She was like a boxer, drawing quick recovering breaths between exchanges.

'Oh, I've heard the name. It's just that we never met. To tell you the truth, Mr Preston, that hobby of Honoria's was something very personal to her. She never discussed it at all. She would just go off by herself for hours on end, and work away at it. I never intruded, and neither did Franklin – that's her husband – because it seemed to represent an entirely private area of her life. Something she escaped into. Can you understand that?'

I nodded, like a man who could understand that.

'Yes, I see. What was she trying to escape from?'

73

The dark flush on her face came and went in under a second.

'Oh, that's just a figure of speech. I meant to say, that was her private place, a hidey-hole if you like. We all have to get away sometimes, don't we? I'm sure the professor would understand the way she felt.'

There was that ball again, zinging back into my half of the field.

'I'm sure he would. He's keenly aware of the importance of her work. That is why he wanted to see it. Still wants to. He had given her an undertaking that if the quality was as high as he thought it might be, he would see about an exhibition. It could lead to fame, in the world of miniatures. It could also make the collection extremely valuable.'

I didn't want to leave it at fame. People can be very dismissive about fame, particularly as applied to somebody else. Money is very different. Nobody shrugs that off. Juliet Freeman was struggling now, as her face clearly showed.

'Well, I really don't know,' she flustered. 'I don't think Franklin would want anyone touching her things—'

'Oh come now Miss Freeman,' I objected, 'there's a possibility that Honoria Lockhart's name could rank among the great miniature painters. As her dear friend, I'm sure you would want that for her?'

She nodded frantically.

'Oh yes. Yes, of course. It would be wonderful. It's just that I don't think I could authorise anything like

74

that. I'd expected your visit to be something more straightforward. This is too much altogether. Only Franklin could deal with this. He's very sensitive about her belongings, you see.'

I turned away, disappointed. 'Ah well, then I'll have to come again after all. Would tonight be too soon, do you think? About eight?'

She looked at her watch, working out how long the grieving widower would need to sleep it off.

'Could you make it nine?'

'Nine o'clock,' I confirmed. 'Please don't bother to see me out. I hope Mr Lockhart will be feeling well enough, by then.'

She walked behind me to the door, as if to ensure that I really went away. I went out to the car, drove to the end of the road, and settled down to wait. Ten minutes later, she emerged from the house, climbed into the little white car, and sped away. I followed her across town, to an apartment block near the beach. She parked in a reserved slot, and went into the building. I gave her a two-minute start, then walked inside and checked the cards in the hallway. No. 207 read "Miss J. Freeman".'

Satisfied, I went back to my own car, and drove around to police headquarters.

Time to report progress to one John Rourke.

SIX

John Rourke received me with that open-handed Irish hospitality for which he is so justly unrenowned.

Looking up from his work, to snarl at the intruder, he changed it to a low keening sound when he saw who it was. He leaned back his head and rolled his eyes towards the Great Policeman in the Sky.

'Where did I go wrong?' he implored.

'Now John,' I placated, 'this won't take a minute. Just doing my duty as a citizen. There are a few things you should know.'

He glared at me unlovingly.

'I know too many things already. What I need right now is a photograph and description of this cowboy who shot up two people at the harbor last night. Do you have it with you?'

'Well, not right off-hand—' I began.

'—never mind. I'll settle for the whereabouts of three teenage hoodlums who raped and murdered a twelve-year-old girl at South Beach yesterday afternoon. Anything?'

'Not just at the moment. What I'm here for—'

'—what you are here for is to tell me a whole lot of stuff I don't want to hear, about some lady's death which wasn't murder in the first place. Try to see it from my point of view, won't you? What I got here is real

76

murders. With bodies and guilty parties and all that stuff. All you bring me is suspicions and wraiths. And what's that?'

'What's what?'

He clicked his tongue impatiently.

'That bag you're holding at your side. Did you bring me an apple?'

That's one of Rourke's troubles. He always goes charging in, getting to the heart of things before people are ready.

'Oh, this,' I held the bag in front of me.

The grizzled head nodded sourly.

'It's the only bag I can see.'

'Well, as a matter of fact, I was going to get round to that—'

'—get round to it now. Give.'

I put the bag on the table and he peered inside.

'You bring me a glass?' he said in disbelief. 'You bring an Irishman an empty glass? That's an insult.'

'No, no John. This one is special. It has fingerprints on it.'

'So it's a dirty, empty glass. Where'd it come from?'

'Just let me tell it my own way,' I begged. 'I've been following up on this Lockhart case—'

'—if it is a case—'

'—and I think it might be. Here's what I've been doing.'

I summarised for him very briefly what I'd been up to since I last saw him. His eyes were closed, as though he was half asleep, but at least he didn't interrupt.

'So you bring me his fingerprints. Why?'

'Well, here's this woman, this Juliet Freeman, very intimate with a man whose wife was buried only last week—'

'—wrong,' he interrupted, 'not buried. Cremated. The lady was cremated. Well, what about this Freeman woman?'

I was a little unsettled by the interruption.

'Like I said,' I continued, 'She walks around the house as if she owns the place. She sent Lockhart off to bed, so that I wouldn't see him drunk.'

Rourke shook his head.

'What is all this? Certainly, she sent the man to bed. Who wouldn't? He wouldn't have been able to hold a proper conversation, so he was best out of the way. She told you herself she was a friend of the wife's. Why shouldn't she know her way around? You're chasing shadows, Preston.'

'Then why did she call him Joe on the phone?' I insisted. 'There's no way you can get Joe out of a name like Franklin Lockhart.'

'Pah,' he sneered. 'Names. What do they mean? Maybe the man hates his name. Lotta people do. They pick one they like better. For all we know, his own wife could have called him Joe. Jevver think of that?'

I hadn't, and my face must have said so. In any case, it was a little late to be asking whether the late Honoria had a pet name for her husband.

'I went to some trouble to get these prints,' I said doggedly. 'I'd like to have them run through.'

78

'So the man has fingerprints,' he scoffed. 'Well, I've got news for you. Every little old lady has a set. So does every child. That doesn't make them Jack the Ripper.'

'We wouldn't know if they were,' I pointed out. 'The Ripper's prints are not on our records.'

Suddenly he was tired of it, or of me.

'If I run these, will you get off my back? Will you go away and let me get after some real criminals?'

'Gladly.'

'OK. I'll put the boy scout on to it. Come back in a couple hours. Oh, and Preston—'

'Yes John?'

'When you come back, ask for the boy. Not me. One thing you haven't told me. I expect it slipped your memory. How'd you make out with the Faro Queen?'

If it was some kind of game, he'd lost me.

'The who?'

'The Faro Queen,' he repeated, with more emphasis. 'Rowena Parker. That's what the boys used to call her in the old days.'

I'll swear he does it deliberately.

'All right, John,' I admitted. 'So I don't know what you're talking about. Why did they call her that?'

He grinned, enjoying himself.

'Didn't they tell you about that? Rowena Parker was the biggest lady gambler on the whole coast, before she retired. Not from old age, you must understand. She couldn't have been more than forty years old at the time. According to her, she'd had enough. Always winning fortunes, and losing 'em just as fast. Then one day, she took a peek in the bank and decided it was time to call it quits. She was on one of her lucky streaks, and just felt it ought to be the last one. So she quit cold. Retired. Just like that. Smart lady, that one. Rich lady, too.'

It had cleared up something that had puzzled me from the outset. I hadn't been able to work out how Honoria's unmarried sister could have come by her reputed wealth. Now. I had the answer.

'This is all new to me,' I admitted, 'and I never heard of anybody called the Faro Queen.'

'Fore your time,' he said condescendingly. 'Matter of fact, it was almost before my time, too. I was just a rookie cop when Rowena was riding high. Knew all about her, of course. Everybody did. She was quite a character. Bet on anything. She would wager a thousand dollars on the color of the shirt of the next man to walk into a bar. But the cards were her real meat. She once bet forty thousand dollars on one hand, just one hand can you imagine? Lost, too. But she came back. She always came back. There was no holding Rowena down.'

'But once she quit, she stayed quit?'

'Right. Nobody believed it would last. They gave her six months, a year. Then she'd come roaring back to the tables. Only she never did. She just took the money and sat on it.'

He spoke with the affectionate recall of happier days. That usually means younger days, and I didn't think Rourke was any exception.

'Good looking woman, was she?' I asked innocently. To my surprise he shook his head.

'No. No I wouldn't say that, exactly. Not good looking. Not like a movie star or a pin-up girl. That wasn't her style. But when she came into a room, you looked, and you kept on looking. Somehow, all the other women just seemed like dolls. There was only Rowena. I'm surprised you haven't bothered to catch up with her.'

Having heard his description of her, I was surprised myself. Until I recalled she was now about seventy years old. Even so, I would have to find a moment to make contact with this living legend.

'It hasn't seemed necessary,' I told him. 'But I don't think I ought to miss the opportunity. Shall I give her your regards?'

'Nah,' he shrugged. 'She wouldn't remember me. She wouldn't remember anybody below the rank of mayor. The high-rollers, that was Rowena's arena. Hey, that isn't bad, huh? Rowena's arena?'

'It's terrible,' I assured him. 'And if you don't treat me right, I'll repeat it to her. But thanks for the tip. I'll be calling on that lady.'

When I left him, I had two hours to spare before calling back to find out the results of my enquiries on Lockhart's fingerprints. There was a certain painting lying on the rear seat of my car. A trip to Professor d'Agostini would just about fill in the time-space.

This trip, I was able to drive direct to the house. The first stars were beginning to appear in a darkening sky, and there were lights on inside. At least the man was home. He had the door open before I could locate a bell-push.

81

'Heard the car-door,' he explained, smiling. 'I didn't expect to see you again, quite so soon, Mr Preston.'

I stood there, with the painting under my arm. He couldn't take his eyes off it.

'Mind if I come in, professor?'

'My dear sir, of course not. How ill-mannered of me to keep you standing out here. Come in, come in.'

We went back into the same comfortable room. There were some heavy leather-bound books lying open, and evidently the man had been working.

'Look, I'm sorry to interrupt, and I promise not to stay more than five minutes. Just wanted you to have this.'

I handed over my prize. He didn't exactly snatch it, but he took it eagerly.

'Ah.' He unrolled it with great care. 'I'm very relieved you didn't fold it, Mr Preston. Some people – well, you'd be amazed at the way they treat things.'

He waved me to sit down, without taking his eyes off the picture.

'H'm. It's very interesting,' he mused. 'Did you pick this one for any special reason, or wasn't there any choice?'

I felt as though he'd caught me out.

'Tell you the truth, professor, there was a choice,' I confessed. 'That one somehow made me think of Honoria Lockhart.'

His eyes twinkled.

'May one ask why?'

The picture showed a man in a long robe seated at a desk. He had been writing something in a book which lay open in front of him, but was interrupted by a figure in the top right-hand corner, which I had taken to represent the Angel of Death. Certainly, the intruder had wings, and seemed to be wielding some kind of chopper.

'The man at the desk is using a pen or a brush, and he seems to be interrupted by death,' I explained lamely. 'Sort of like the dead lady, in a way.'

The professor nodded, satisfied.

'Yes. Yes. I see what you mean. Very good indeed, Mr Preston, if you don't mind my saying so. Most apt. And the picture itself, of course, is very famous. It is early eleventh century, from what we term the Winchester School. Originally from the Grimbald Gospels. The seated figure is St Matthew, of course. The original is in the British Museum, London. I have inspected it many times.'

I didn't want to risk another lecture like the last one, so I said quickly 'Is it any good?'

He looked offended.

'Any good? It's priceless, Mr Preston. Quite beyond price. They are not in the habit of storing rubbish in the British Museum.'

It was my own fault, I realised.

'No, sir, that's wasn't my question. I meant the picture in your hand. Mrs Lockhart's work. Is it a good reproduction?'

'Ah,' he nodded, mollified. 'I see what you mean. Any good? Well now, let's see.'

He carried it across to a small table, snapping on a reading light and smoothing the picture out beneath it.

There was a long silence, and I began to wonder whether he had forgotten I was there. Several times he said 'h'm', and I thought he was about to speak, but then he would follow with 'ah' and resume his inspection. Finally, he straightened up, and looked at me almost absently.

'Remarkable,' he breathed. 'Truly remarkable. There would need to be tests, of course.'

'Tests,' I repeated, trying to look like a man who understands.

'Oh yes, many tests. It's quite incredible, you know, the way in which science has come to the aid of the scholars in these matters. Left to ourselves, we would argue back and forth for years. Used to, in fact, until the last half of the present century. Now we have all this scientific equipment. We can pinpoint the age of both paint and paper, with quite remarkable accuracy. Also the chemical constituents of the paint. Many a clever forger has been unmasked in that way.'

'Forgers, yes,' said the intelligent audience.

'With paint you see, the ancients could only use the materials of their time. Crude dyes and so forth. A modernist might be able to create the appearance of the old works, but the texture is another matter entirely. That is where Mrs Lockhart's work appears so unusual. She seems to have come very close, not to copying, but to reproducing the original work. Just on a visual inspection, you understand.'

'I quite understand.'

'There must be tests, as I say. But even so, it is something of a tour-de-force. Remarkable is the only word. You say there are others? Locked up in a safe place, I trust?'

I thought of the cardboard boxes under the bed, but I couldn't bring myself to tell him that.

'I believe they are quite safe,' I assured him.

'Well, I just hope so. You know Mr Preston, I am not an excitable kind of person, but I cannot restrain myself entirely. This discovery could put Mrs Lockhart into a very particular niche in my world. A small world, I grant you, but not without a certain status, I believe.'

'You mean the work could be valuable?'

I really must learn to choose my words with more care around this man, I realised at once.

'Valuable,' he repeated scornfully. 'Well, you know, I fancy that word has different meanings according to who is saying it. I take it you are asking whether this beautiful work would be worth a lot in terms of dollars and cents? I don't know the answer. The value to scholars would be very small. This is, after all, only a copy. It is the original that matters. A private collector, an enthusiast, might be interested in purchase. There would be an undeniable attraction in owning for oneself a reproduction of such quality. As to what such a person would pay, well who can tell? I, for example, might go as high as one hundred dollars. A poor return for the hundreds of hours of painstaking effort put into the work.'

Poor indeed, I reflected. But then, the professor was himself poor, in money terms. It was probably all he could afford. Plus, he clearly had a low opinion of the market place. For a more enlightened view, I would have to go to Joshua Holland.

'Well, thank you for your time, professor,' I said, rising. 'I really ought to be getting along.'

He stood in front of the painting, as if I might be going to steal it.

'You'll leave this with me?' he queried. 'I can hardly wait to get my laboratory friends on to it.'

I hesitated, not wanting to shock him.

'This is a little difficult for me to say,' I told him. 'But I'll have to ask you to keep the artist's name confidential.'

'Really? Why?'

'The fact is, professor, her husband didn't want me to have it in the first place. Didn't want her memory disturbed, was what he said. But it seemed to me he was being dog-in-the-manger about it. After all, if his late wife had produced something that would interest the world at large, I thought it would be what she would want, if she were around to be consulted.'

'So you stole it,' he announced flatly.

'I wouldn't put it like that,' I hedged. 'I don't want to keep it, or anything. I simply wanted to get your opinion on it, that was all. I always intended to put it back. I still do.'

He stared at me with what I took to be disapproval. Then the look dissolved, and he beamed.

'Quite right too,' he approved. 'Exactly what I would have done, in your place, Mr Lockhart should be very grateful to you, as indeed I am. I shall explain it to him myself.'

That was more approval than I needed at that moment.

'Very kind, professor, and I'll take you up on that offer. But not for a while, if you please. Let's just keep this between you and me, for the moment. I'd like to pick my time before mentioning it to him again. He's still grieving, you understand.'

The professor nodded furiously.

'Quite understand. Poor man. Yes, we must be very circumspect. Very well, I will leave it to you. In the meantime, I will proceed with the tests, and wait to hear from you.'

We shook hands, like the fine conspirators we were, and I left him. Driving through the darkening streets, I realised I was only a few blocks away from Rowena Parker's address. It would avoid an extra journey if I were to call on that lady now. On the other hand, there should be some information waiting for me at headquarters. Fortunately, there is a thing called the telephone. I cruised along, looking for a pay-booth, spotted one and pulled in. When I got through to headquarters, I asked for Detective Henry Larsen. After a search at the other end, they announced that he was out. No, they didn't know what time he would be back, and no, there was no message for anybody called Preston. I asked for a note to be left on his desk, saying I had tried to contact him, and would call in later.

Five minutes afterward, I was drawing into the kerb, outside the address occupied by the one-time Faro Queen.

SEVEN

I didn't know that section of town very well, but I was mildly surprised when I found Miss Parker's place. Sheila Fyffe had spoken in terms of a big old house in the Heights district. Well, this was the Heights district, and there were still quite a few of those places around, but not where Rowena Parker lived. I was looking at a solid old apartment block, built in the days when ten stories was considered dangerous. Mrs Fyffe's information had already proved to be wrong in so many ways that I ought to quit feeling surprised.

Inside, I caught a familiar smell, and I knew it at once. It was called money. Even the security guard wore a proper suit and a tie, and described himself as the manager.

'Miss Parker? Oh yes. That's the lady in six o seven. She's expecting you, is she?'

'No,' I replied. 'She doesn't even know me.'

He didn't like that at all, and braced all over, quite perceptibly.

'If you'll just give me your name. I'll check whether the lady will see you,' he said frostily.

'The name is Preston,' I began, then stopped when he clicked his fingers.

'Sure it is,' he agreed. 'Thought I knew you. Private

John, right?'

'Right,' I agreed, 'but I don't think—'

'Phil Page,' he went on. 'I was twenty years in the old Eighth Precinct. That was before I retired, naturally. They were good days, the Eighth. Sure, I remember you. Well, how're things?'

Things were fine with me, and things were fine with him, and one thing seemed to lead to another. There isn't a great deal for a security guard to do, watching somebody's front door, and I made a welcome break in Page's routine. He'd held the job for three years now, he confided, and the most he'd had to do was to turn away salesmen. Not a very active life for a man who'd spent his vigorous years in the police force.

'What kind of a lady is Miss Parker?' I asked innocently.

His face became a mask at once. 'Very nice lady. Always with the "good morning" and all that stuff. Nice lady. All my people are nice people.'

And that, I was to understand, was the end of that. I grinned.

'Well, how about telling the nice lady there's a nice feller down here? Tell her it's about her late sister's estate.'

'Gotcha.'

He went behind the tiny counter and plugged into the switchboard. She evidently asked him a question, because he said

'Oh yes, Miss Parker, I used to know him myself, when I was on the force. Right. Thank you.'

Breaking off the connection, he looked across at me, nodding.

'Six o seven. She says to go up.'

There was only one elevator, an ornate, old-fashioned affair, with elaborate iron grille work and a sliding gate you had to push yourself. But it gave a surprisingly smooth ride, and stopped at six with none of the clanking I was anticipating. Stepping out into a broad corridor, I followed the numbered arrows, and was soon pulling a gold-painted bell-handle.

She made me wait a few moments, then the door opened slowly, and I got my first look at Rowena Parker. She held her five foot six very straight, and clear eyes inspected me from a face which had resisted the time ravages remarkably well. The immaculate bouffant hair was an obvious wig.

'Mr Preston?'

'How do you do Miss Parker. I'd like to have a few words, if you can spare me the time. It's about your late sister—'

'Yes, yes,' she clucked, 'Mr Page told me. Well, you'd better come in, I suppose.'

We went into a room where everything seemed to be covered in chintz.

'Take that chair there, please.'

I sat dutifully down, and waited while she composed herself carefully on a facing seat.

'Now then, Mr Preston, what's all this about dear Honoria?'

It was the first time I'd seen her hands. Long and finely

90

shaped, with slim tapering fingers that could have belonged to a violinist. I tried to visualise a pack of playing cards being riffled expertly between them, and it wasn't difficult.

"Well ma'am, did she ever talk to you about her hobby?'

She held herself erect in the chair, so that she was practically looking at me down her nose.

'Hobby? Do you mean that painting business? What about it?'

Evidently my hostess wasn't very impressed with what she called the painting business. Nor with me, either, so far.

'That's what I've come to see you about,' I explained. 'You see, your sister was in touch with an expert, a professor out at Berkeley. He's a very prominent man, and he thinks her work is of a very high standard.'

She didn't exactly sniff, but she wasn't enthusiastic either.

'Well, what of it?'

'The fact is, he thinks your sister's work could easily win some kind of recognition. It's that good.'

There was a glimmer of interest now. Recognition could mean money, and Rowena knew about money.

'That's very interesting. It would be nice for her. But tell me, why didn't this professor say all this before? Why wait until my sister died?'

The years had obviously not slowed her mental processes.

'They'd sort of lost touch lately,' I told her. 'He hadn't

realised how much progress Mrs Lockhart had made. He's very enthusiastic, believe me.'

She smoothed at her floor-length dress.

'I see no reason either to believe you or disbelieve you. Mr Preston. What I want to know is, why have you come to me?'

Which is what we call, in the trade, a valid question. And it brought me right into the delicate area of family politics.

'Fact is, Mr Lockhart seems reluctant to cooperate.'

'H'm. That creature. You've spoken to him then?'

'No,' I confessed, 'not directly. I went out to the house to see him, but he wasn't well.'

Her eyes narrowed at that.

'Then how do you know he won't cooperate?'

If Miss Parker even needed a job, she would have found a place on an investigating team.

'There's this friend of your sister's, a Mrs Fyffe, you may have met her.'

'No,' she denied, 'but Honoria has mentioned her name.'

There was no shading of emphasis in her reply to indicate whether Sheila Fyffe merited a good or a bad rating.

'Well, Mrs Fyffe asked if she could have one piece of Honoria's work as a kind of keepsake. Mr Lockhart refused. He said he wouldn't have her things desecrated, or some such thing.'

Rowena shook her head.

'I doubt whether he said that,' she observed. 'I doubt

whether Mr Lockhart's vocabulary extends to a word like desecrate. However, the point is, he refused. And now you're here to see if you can get me to change his mind. Is that it?'

She had a way of getting to the point, which some people might find disconcerting. I was one of those people.

'I was hoping you might be able to use your influence, yes.'

'Influence,' she scoffed. 'I have none at all, I assure you. The only influence that man understands is money. That was why he married Honoria in the first place, you know. Thought she had money. Well, he got quite a surprise.'

If she was right, then Lockhart had certainly made a big mistake. It had been lucky for Rowena that he didn't see her first, I reflected. But what she had just said provided me with a new lead-in.

'I don't know him of course,' I said blandly, 'so I really couldn't make any comment. Money though, I know about that. It's possible that your sister's work could be worth money. I would have thought, from what you say, that Mr Lockhart would at least want to hear more about the possibility.'

She was staring away from me, thinking.

'Yes,' she agreed, 'that is strange. Out of character. You ought to ask him again. Or rather, for the first time. I gather your information so far is at second hand?'

'That is true. Well, I am intending to see him this evening. She said I ought to try at nine o'clock.'

Finely-pencilled eyebrows were raised.

'She? You mean Mrs Fyffe is over at the house? Whatever for?'

It was an understandable assumption. I shook my head.

'No, not Mrs Fyffe. Another friend of your sister's. A Miss Freeman.'

I was watching her expression as I spoke, looking for some spark of recognition of the name. There was none.

'Freeman? I don't recall that name. Still,' she opened the splendid hands, 'there is no reason why I should. My sister and I did not exactly live in each other's pockets. She had her own friends, and that is as it should be.'

I accepted this gravely.

'Of course. Miss Freeman seemed a very nice young woman. She told me Honoria was like a mother to her.'

By now, I was beginning to appreciate why Rowena had been such a successful gambler. Her face seldom gave any hints to the opposition as to what kind of cards she was holding. She had a system. All new information was taken in and considered for a full ten seconds, while she decided on what facial expression should next be registered. It was a very short interval, but long enough for her to retain control. There was no instantaneous flash, nothing to inform the watcher.

This time she decided on mild surprise.

'A mother? Well, that's the first time I ever heard that description applied. Honoria had many fine qualities, but she never had any motherly instincts. We were alike in that respect, at least. Your Miss Freeman sounds like

94

a rather impressionable young woman. A dependent type, would you say?'

I half-smiled.

'No I wouldn't. Quite the reverse. The lady struck me as being well able to take care of herself. It would be hard to imagine anyone less in need of a mother. She seemed to know how to deal with your brother-in-law, and I didn't hear him argue.'

'Please don't describe that man as my brother-in-law,' she returned tetchily. 'And what do you mean when you say she dealt with him?'

'She put him to bed,' I said, and I didn't bother being gentle. 'He was drunk out of his head.'

'I see.' She spoke evenly, as though this new information came as no news. 'Well, this is all very interesting, Mr Preston, but I don't think it really leads us anywhere. The point is, you are going to see Mr Lockhart this evening. If he still refuses to let your friend the professor have access to Honoria's work, you would like me to use any influence I may have. That is the situation, am I correct?'

I was being told it was time to leave, so I got up.

'That's it, Miss Parker. Perhaps I could telephone you, and let you know what happens?'

'Please do. But leave it until morning. I'm not one for staying up late in the evening these days.'

If that was her recipe for maintaining a youthful appearance, it certainly worked. Promising to call her 'not before ten, please', I made my way back downstairs. Phil Page was deep in a lurid-colored paperback. As I

95

approached, he looked up.

'You all through?'

As a pointless question, it surely qualified for some kind of prize.

'Just about,' I confirmed. 'Nice lady.'

'You got it,' he agreed. 'Never no fuss, know what I mean? 'Tween you and me, they're not all like her. I got one or two here, nothing is ever right, you know? But not her, not Miss Parker. Fast with a dollar, too.'

'Really? Must come in handy around Christmas.'

'Could be,' he shrugged. 'All I know, I kind of kept an eye on the removal squad when she moved in. Courtesy of the house. She spread me a twenty for that. She didn't have to. It was nice of her.'

'Some people appreciate things,' I observed fatuously. 'Well, I'll be seeing you.'

I decided against phoning headquarters. I had to pass the place anyway on my way back to Parkside. There was a different duty sergeant on the desk, and he didn't know me. He also didn't think it was possible anybody could want Probationer-Detective Larsen.

'You sure you got that right?' he queried.

'Absolutely,' I assured him. 'Henry Larsen.'

'I don't know whether he's supposed to handle visitors,' he objected. 'Larsen is what you might call kind of a student, you know?'

'I know. I also know John Rourke told me himself that Larsen would be dealing with things.'

'Rourke said that?' He sounded doubtful.

'Word for word,' I confirmed. 'But you don't have to

take it from me. The phone's beside you. Check it with Rourke.'

He didn't like the idea. The Irishman's irascibility was famous. If he thought his orders were being questioned by some desk-sergeant, the sergeant might find himself unable to sit down for the remainder of the shift.

'Well,' he grumbled, caving in, 'I guess if that's what the captain said, that's what he said.'

'That's what he said,' I contributed, making it unanimous.

He picked up the phone, stabbing buttons, then muttered into it.

'You're in luck,' he announced, clearly against his will. 'Larsen just got back in ten minutes ago. He's upstairs right now. Do you know your way?'

'Oh yes,' I said dolefully. 'All too well.'

I trudged up those battered stairs again, walking past Rourke's private domain, and making for the squad room. The squad, at that moment, consisted of one apprentice detective with a bright and eager face. He was obviously waiting for me.

'Ah, Mr Preston. We meet again.'

You couldn't help liking the guy. He was all bounce and energy, like some tail-wagging puppy.

'That we do, Henry.'

I perched on one of the villainous chairs, evidently made by the same homicide-inclined carpenter as the ones in Rourke's office. Digging around for my Old Favorites, I held out the pack.

He was horrified.

'Not me. Don't you know what those things do to your insides? I have seen color slides that would make your hair curl.'

I received this information calmly, through a cloud of exhaled smoke.

'Yeah, I know. It took them hours to get those pictures right. I'm supposed to collect a royalty, you know.'

He paused, then gulped, then grinned. Watching his face was like watching a camera shutter clicking.

'That's interesting. When I first sniffed those things Mr Rourke smokes, I thought he must have provided the slides.'

'Better not let him hear you,' I counselled. 'Well now, how about those smudges? Do we win a prize?'

He wiped off the grin, regarding me seriously.

'Matter of fact, Mr Preston, you seem to have found something.'

And if I wanted to know what it was, I was going to have to push.

'Fine. What kind of something?'

He scratched at the unruly hair.

'What will you do with this information?' he parried.

'Hard to say, unless I know what it is,' I pointed out, reasonably. 'It's just that I'm very interested in Franklin Lockhart. His wife died an accidental death, and I'm poking around wherever I can. There are people who don't go for that accident definition.'

'What people?'

I looked at him severely.

'Oh no. The law is quite clear about that. I don't have

98

to reveal the names of my clients, not at this stage anyway. Didn't they tell you all that stuff?'

It was so long since I had needed to remind a police officer of that particular piece of legislation, I'd almost forgotten the formula.

Larsen flushed slightly.

'Naturally,' he snapped. Then, by way of emphasis, 'of course. Well, I wouldn't know about any accidental death. That file is closed, and there the matter ends so far as the department is concerned.'

'Not quite,' I contradicted.

'How's that?'

'I said "not quite",' I repeated. 'I promised your boss I would let him have any information I came up with. Closed files can be re-opened, you know. It looks better to the taxpayers if it gets re-opened by this department, rather than by some private citizen. Even if he does have a license. That's why I made my deal with John.'

It seemed an appropriate moment to remind him that it was first names between his boss and me. Some of the starch went out of him.

'Oh, I hadn't quite appreciated that.'

'Well, I'm sure you understand now,' I smiled easily. 'So how about the prints? What's their story?'

'They have quite a tale to tell,' he informed me. 'It seems that Mr Franklin Lockhart isn't Mr Franklin Lockhart at all. The Franklin is OK but it's the surname. Joseph P. Franklin is what it says on the file.'

'Uh huh. Is he wanted for anything?'

I looked impressed, while I recalled that Juliet Freeman had called him Joe.

'A little,' hedged Larsen. This was a big scene for him, and he wasn't going to waste it. 'Mr Franklin used to be in the army, but he didn't care for it, so he quit. It was kind of informal. What he did was, he loaded up a big truck with all kinds of equipment, and just drove off with it one day. The army have a poor opinion of Mr Franklin, I'm afraid to say.'

'They can be very stuffy about that kind of thing,' I acknowledged. 'When was all this?'

'Three years ago. Then, just over two years ago, they caught up with him. In Montana. Seems he'd entered into a form of marriage with some elderly woman over there and was leading the quiet life. Just by bad luck, one of his old outfit was on leave, and happened to spot him. That started a row between the army and the local police. Seems he didn't have any right to get married to this lady, because he was already married to another party and it must have slipped his mind.'

'So the local boys wanted him for bigamy, and the army wanted him for desertion, and theft, and Lord knows what else. Who got him in the end?'

Larsen spread his hands, sighing.

'Nobody. They put Mr Franklin in the local hoosegow while all the authorities argued about jurisdiction and so forth. Mr Franklin got bored with waiting for a decision, so he left. On his way out, he shot a constable, and the constable died. There's a lot of people want to talk to your Mr Franklin. Matter of fact, the army is sending some people over. Could be here any time now.'

100

I ground out the Old Favorite, thinking. Joe Franklin had obviously been a very busy man these last few years. It seemed to confirm Sheila Fyffe's opinion of him, and it didn't make me any happier about Honoria's death.

'But you have the first grab, right?' I asked. 'Obviously, you have another case of bigamy right here in Monkton. That makes it your pinch, doesn't it?'

'You'll need a higher authority than me to decide that one,' he returned.

I couldn't understand why he seemed to be taking everything so calmly. Somebody should be rushing around, waving handcuffs.

'But you can't just leave him walking around, while somebody makes a decision,' I protested.

'I'm surprised at your low opinion of us, Mr Preston,' he chided. 'We've got an A and D out on him right now. I've already been out to the house, but he wasn't there. Car's missing from the garage. Doesn't look as though he's actually pulled out, though. All his clothes are there, all his personal stuff. We ought to pick him up before the night's out. I'm afraid this puts you out of a job, though.'

My surprise was not assumed.

'Why do you say that? Seems to me what you've done is to provide me with a suspect made to measure.'

He nodded.

'Yeah, but it hardly matters, does it? You would have the devil's own job to prove that Mrs Lockhart's death was a homicide, in the first place. And even then, you'd have just as much trouble in establishing that this Franklin killed her. Why would he want to? There was no profit there, no money. The lady's death was an inconvenience to him. Here he was, all set up in a nice quiet way of life. Nothing much to do, no problems. Why should he go and spoil all that? It doesn't seem to make an awful lot of sense, you must agree.'

I didn't want to agree. I didn't want them taking away my nice fat murder-suspect. It was just me being childish, really. Joe Franklin, as I must now think of him, was going to have to answer for a whole tally of earlier crimes. Come to think of it, with so many cards stacked against him, it really didn't matter a damn whether he had killed Honoria or not. He was already going to take the big fall for that Montana police officer's death.

Could it be that I was getting petty? What did I care who arrested him, so long as he got what was coming? Where did I stand in all this? I was acting like some kid who didn't score the winning goal himself. The team won, didn't they? My team, the good guys? Why did I always have to be the headliner, the crowd-pleaser? And I mustn't let my resentment show in front of this rookie.

'No, I guess you're right,' I agreed. 'Doesn't seem to be much in this for me, not now. I'll probably just clear up a couple of loose ends, make out my report, and wind it up. Thanks for putting me in the picture, Henry. Appreciate that.'

'It's for me to thank you,' he pointed out. 'if you hadn't brought that glass in here, old Joe might just have got away with it all.'

'Always glad to help the department,' I glad-handed.

'Hope you get him soon.'

'Rely on it.'

I went back out into the night, deep in thought.

EIGHT

Probationer Detective Henry Larsen might be a new-comer to the Homicide Bureau, but that didn't make him an amateur. He seemed to be shaping up pretty well to his new environment, and there was no room for any doubt that he had warned me off the Lockhart case. He had not yet acquired the Rourke technique, or the Rourke dialogue, but these would follow. In the mean-time, his own approach was just as positive, if less direct.

Strictly speaking, there was no special reason why I should carry on, warning or no. Whether or not Joe Franklin had eased the unfortunate Honoria off this mortal coil had become rather academic. He was already wanted for so much misbehavior, including murder one, that they were going to throw the book at him in any case. If you looked at it in round terms, justice was going to be done, and that ought to satisfy everybody, includ-ing me.

But it didn't.

I still wanted to know, to understand. Why had Hon-oria died? There was no profit in it for Franklin, and in fact quite the reverse. It took away his nice quiet hidey-hole, and put him back out on the street. That was an aspect I hadn't been able to explain from the outset, but it was made doubly inconsistent by the new information

Larsen had given me. The only possible answer seemed to relate to Juliet Freeman. She was young and attractive, and she called him Joe. That could mean she knew him from the past.

I sat in the car, and brooded on the girl, trying to explain Franklin's actions in the light of her existence. Supposing, just supposing that Juliet had arrived in Monkton City quite by chance, and run into her old buddy Joe Franklin. Supposing they'd had a thing going at one time, and had started up again when they re-met? That could explain many things, probably everything. It would explain why Honoria had become a nuisance, and nuisances tend to be dealt with only one way by a man with the kind of past history Joe Franklin had. It would explain why he wasn't concerned about losing his roof, if Juliet was willing and able to provide an alternative. I didn't like it, especially, but there is one golden rule that a man in my business always has to keep bright and shining in the forefront of his mind. If there is a dame involved, there is no need to explain every bit of a man's behavior in rational terms. The most logical and clear-thinking man will do the most outrageous things, make the most ridiculous mistakes, if there is a woman in the background. I don't know who it was who first came up with the phrase 'cherchez la femme', but I'll bet he was a copper.

It could also explain why Mr Franklin was not receiving guests when Detective Larsen called at the house, and my call could have been responsible, at least in part. Joe Franklin may have been belting away at the sauce, but Juliet Freeman was a clear-headed a gal as you could wish to meet. She might have decided that it was time for Joe to move on. I could mean some kind of publicity, with all my chatter about Professor d'Agostini and the paintings, and the last thing either of them wanted was to be in the spotlight. If I was right, then she'd certainly saved him, even though her reasons had been wrong. I was getting to like my reasoning more and more. If Juliet had been the woman behind the curtains, then nobody would know about her. Joe Franklin would simply walk out of the house on Montenero Drive, and vanish. the police would not begin to know where to look for him. As for me, I wasn't anybody much. Just a man who would call at the house at nine o'clock, and find it empty. I'd be annoyed, naturally, but it would hardly cause me to complain to the police. No, I would simply try again next day, and the day after that. Then, in all probability, I would simply give up.

Then I thought of my client, Sheila Fyffe.

As a frequent visitor to the house, and one-time confidante of the deceased Honoria, she had been in a close position to observe what went on. It was not impossible that she might know something about Juliet Freeman. If she did, then she was probably the only living person who could put a line from Joe Franklin in that direction. That made her a risk, and people like Franklin cannot afford risks of that kind.

I found a bar with a row of pay-phones at the rear, and called up my client. She didn't sound very grateful.

'Mr Preston?' she repeated in disbelief. 'Do you know

what time it is? It's almost ten o'clock at night.'

She made it sound like the official starting hour for some devil's orgy.

'Yes,' I said apologetically, 'sorry about this, Mrs Fyffe, but it could be important.'

'Have you found something?' she jumped in eagerly.

'Quite a lot has happened,' I reported, 'but the important thing is, I don't want you to get alarmed.'

'Why would I get alarmed?' she demanded. 'Really, Mr Preston, it's too exasperating of you. What is going on?'

If only she would stop interrupting me, I would be able to get around to that.

'It's about Lockhart,' I explained. 'The man is a fugitive.'

She snapped it up with triumph.

'I knew it,' she chortled. 'I knew it.'

'No, just a moment, let me explain.'

I told her as briefly as possible about Lockhart/Franklin's past history, with suitable punctuations of 'H'm' and 'Huh' from the other end.

'The reason I'm calling you, Mrs Fyffe, is to warn you. This is a dangerous man we're dealing with, and there's no telling what he might do next. I think you ought to pay special attention to locking up the house, until they catch him.'

'Why? Why should he harm me?'

She didn't sound particularly frightened. Simply interested.

'People on the run don't always think rationally,' I

soothed. 'There's no telling what goes on in their heads. It's just that I think it would do no harm to take elementary precautions. Just for a day or two. The police will pick him up quite soon, I imagine.'

'Huh,' she shorted, but it wasn't clear whether the snort applied to my warning, or to the speed with which the police would find Franklin. 'Well, just you don't worry yourself about me, young man. If that creature comes to this house, I'll know how to deal with him. There's a shotgun in the attic, and I know how to use it.'

A shotgun would certainly improve her chances, I reflected.

'I could easily mention your name to the police,' I suggested. 'They could check on you from time to time.'

There was no room for doubt about the intention of the snort that time.

'No thank you,' she rejected emphatically. 'They'd probably get in my way. You'll let me know what happens, Mr Preston?'

'Rely on it,' I assured her. 'And you'll call if you need me?'

'Agreed.' Then she added brightly 'it's all getting quite exciting, wouldn't you say?'

I couldn't restrain a grin. My opinion of Mrs Sheila Fyffe was going to have to be revised.

'Things are certainly warming up. You take care now.'

Putting down the receiver, I stood musing for a moment.

'Are you through with that phone?'

The interrupter was a fat, sweaty-faced man, who

frowned at me impatiently.

'Sure. Go ahead.'

I went back out into the street. It was quite dark by now, and the sky was, for once, living up to the description given by the tourist bureau. I wondered whether Joe Franklin was also looking at it at that moment, and whether Juliet was helping him. There was only one way to find out.

It was a fifteen minute drive to the Freeman address. I sat outside for a few moments, looking up at the apartment building which had the usual crossword puzzle appearance of light squares and dark squares. Maybe my quarry was sitting up there right now, anxiously watching the newscasts to see if he made the headlines. One thing was certain, he wouldn't be pleased to see me. Reaching under the glove compartment, I carefully peeled off the adhesive plaster which held the spare thirty eight in position. Then I checked it over, in the half-light from a distant street lamp. I'd forgotten once, many years before, to check my weapon before going up against armed opposition. I was lucky that time. All I collected was a slug in the shoulder, but a man can't expect that kind of good fortune more than once. Satisfied, I tucked the gun away, and went across the street. Ignoring the elevators, I opted for the broad stairway and soon found myself on the landing which told me that 201-210 were away to the right. There was loud music coming from 203 and I half-expected an irate neighbour to appear at any moment from one of the adjacent apartments. Nobody came, and soon I was standing outside 207. Standing to one side of the door, I leaned on the buzzer. There was no response, and after a while I tried again, with the same result. Inspecting the door lock, I quickly decided my little bunch of wire skeletons would be non-effective against it. At the end of the corridor, a red fire-door, securely bolted, let out onto the fire escape. Keeping my fingers crossed against any traffic in or out of the other apartments, I went to the red door and put pressure on the big bolts. It's quite usual to find these things rusting in position, as any fire-chief will tell you, but the maintenance people in this particular block were obviously on the ball. The bolts slid easily and noiselessly free, and soon I was through and standing on the metal platform above the street. I had to move to my right, past Apartment 206, which was a blaze of light. Inching my way gingerly along the narrow ledge, I peeked in at the first window. There was no one in view, but someone was evidently not far away, judging by the lights and the television which was going at full blast. The Rick Bradford show was on, and Rick is my very favorite private eye. The things that man can do in fifty-four minutes are enough to make lesser people look for some other line of work. Like then, for instance. There was old Rick, hunched over a pool-side bar with an edible blonde on one side and a ditto redhead on the other. Laughing nymphettes kept diving into the pool, while Rick kept diving into this tall, frosted glass. You didn't catch him crawling along narrow ledges with his heart in his mouth, a long drop to the street below, and a prospective interview with a refugee murderer.

I was thinking unkind thoughts about life in general as I edged towards the second window. There was the tenant of 206, a tall skinny woman busy mixing up something on the stove. She had a whole range of herbs and seasonings within reach, and these were getting plenty of action. Well, she could certainly do with the nourishment, by the look of her. Her face was half towards me, and I didn't dare risk crossing that broad sheet of glass until she moved away. I wished I could see inside the Chinese iron pot she was working on. Whatever it was, there would be no shortage of flavor. There she went again, reaching around for some new ingredient. But it wasn't there. She frowned, and checked the stocks again. Then she crossed over to a cupboard and opened it, peering inside. Her back was to me now, and it was my chance to move. Not taking my eyes off her, I crossed the window as quickly as was safe, pausing at the far side to check that she hadn't spotted me out of the corner of her eye. I needn't have worried. She was far too triumphant in her discovery of the missing ingredient to bother with such trivialities as prowlers.

The window of Apartment 207 stared blankly out at the surrounding night. Spreadeagled against the comfortless concrete, I felt new fear. Behind me, the lighted oblongs had presented problems. Lights meant people, and that in turn meant I had to be careful not to be seen. Lights gave me a sporting chance. People inside could look out and spot me, but I could look in, and see them first. That made it an even contest.

But what did no lights mean?

111

No lights meant that people inside could still look out, but I could not look in. No lights could mean that Joe Franklin, army deserter and cop-killer, was crouched in the darkness, sweating with fear and all set to start shooting at all callers. Franklin was for the big fall when they caught up with him, and guys like that don't wait around for conversation. There was no time for any discussion, just bang bang you're dead. The you in this case being me. In fact, now that I faced the reality, it occurred to me that he needn't even shoot. All he had to do was raise the window, and push. The concrete far below would finish the job.

This may all sound like unproductive thinking, but a man doesn't think at his best in those conditions. Sweat was beginning to roll down my forehead, stinging my eyes, and it wasn't caused by the night heat. Keeping as much of my body as possible clear of the window, I peered around, trying to penetrate the darkness inside the apartment. I couldn't see a thing. If he was in there, you'd think he would at least light a cigarette or something, to even things up. Nothing. It was decisions time. Either I was going in or I wasn't. The thirty eight in my pocket, which had seemed such a comfort when I put it there, was now just useless extra weight. I needed both hands for my inchings and wrigglings. The pocket-knife was another matter. It had a useful job to do. I was halfway across the window now, and had to shut out my fears in order to concentrate on the job in hand. I must make a swell target – no, that wouldn't help at all. Stay with the knife. By leaning my weight against the inhospitable glass I was able to work my left hand down into the pocket of my jacket. My fingers closed around the haft of the knife. Shrugging it free I slid my hand up the glass until it reached the window sash. Gently I slipped the point beneath the divider, and pushed upwards, then sideways at the retaining catch. It wouldn't budge, and the unexpected resistance almost caused me to lose my hold on the haft. My right hand was gripping at the wall face, and I could feel the treacherous sweat working its way along my fingers, imperilling their security. Another push with the knife. This time the catch moved slightly, but did not spring quite clear. My right hand slid down a couple of inches, and I pressed even harder against the window. Fear was now my only motivation. I gave a last savage shove with the blade. The catch snapped free, and I heaved up the window and fell into the room, all in one movement. It took a few seconds for the trembling to go away. Plenty of time for anyone in the apartment to have found me, and do whatever they were about to do. No one came.

Cautiously, I climbed to my feet. There could be no doubt about it. I was alone in the apartment. No one could have failed to hear the crash of my undignified entrance. I walked across the room, banging into things, until I reached the wall. Then I slid my hand along, working it up and down until I found a light-switch. The sudden flood of light made me screw up my eyes, which had been thoroughly tuned in to darkness. I was in what was obviously the living room, with two other doors leading off. The first took me into a small kitchen, where a few dishes were stacked ready for washing. There seemed to be two of everything, so Juliet had had company for the meal. It didn't need a big expensive detective to work out who that might have been. I went through the other door, which had to be the bedroom, and stopped cold in my tracks. I'd been wrong about Joe Franklin. He hadn't been waiting for callers at all. He was too busy being dead.

He lay, sprawled beside the bed, face down on the floor. His right hand was flung outwards as though reaching for the ivory telephone which stood on the bedside table. His bare back was a ragged mess of unsightly black, red-rimmed holes, where at least four slugs had been pumped into him. Somebody was going to have to wash off all that drying blood to find the exact number.

Sitting down on the bed, I pulled out my Old Favorites and lit one, from a shaky flame. Was I letting my imagination run away with me, or had he been making for the phone when he was hit? And who was he going to call? I wasted a couple of minutes on this kind of pointless speculation, then realised that I was really using up time to pull myself back into some kind of rational shape.

The situation was really very simple.

Joe Franklin was dead, murdered. The point at issue was, what was I going to do about it? The simplest thing would be to call the police, but I didn't want to do that. The dead man was on the run, and I'd left police headquarters just a little while before, knowing that. Knowing it, and also knowing where I might find him.

Only I forgot to mention that small item to the law. That was bad enough in itself, but there was more. Franklin hadn't been dead very long. I'm no doctor, but I know how quickly blood coagulates. Some unkind people, and there are few more unkind than the police in a case of homicide, might feel they could have prevented it from happening. If I had told them about Juliet Freeman, and they had sent the local police in at once, maybe Joe Franklin would be alive. On the other hand, you could reason that the Franklin file could now be closed, and regard that as a bonus. But they wouldn't reason that way. I knew. All they would say was that they now had a brand new homicide on their hands, perpetrator unknown. One more reason for disliking me.

Any which way you read it, I was in trouble. The best thing I could do was to dig around on my own account. If I came up with answers, the people at homicide might take a more lenient view of my little memory lapses. The first thing to do was to find Juliet. She hadn't struck me as the kind of person who would fill her boyfriend full of holes, but I've been around too long to let that fool me. The jails are full of people who aren't the kind of people to pull the stunts that put them in there. Especially dame people. Dames can be very unpredictable when thwarted.

Heaving myself up from the bed, I stepped over the late-lamented and began poking around. If Juliet had lammed out, she was travelling very light. The closets were stuffed with clothes, including one sable wrap, carefully tucked away in a paper-lined box. There were also two suitcases in the apartment. Not many people run to three, and those cases made me even more certain of my first thoughts. The lady had either run off in a blind panic, in the clothes she stood up in, or she hadn't run off at all. It was the money that clinched it. There was close to six hundred dollars in cash, at the back of a drawer. Panic or no, people don't leave cash lying around when they take off. Cash is the main ingredient for anybody on the run. Cheque books, credit cards, all the paraphernalia of a settled existence, all become useless overnight. That doesn't happen with folding money.

I closed the drawer thoughtfully, and stared around, willing the place to reveal something that might help me locate the girl. Then I remembered the notepad close to the telephone. Reaching over for it, I almost stepped on Franklin's hand, which made me slightly queasy. In the little book there were several numbers with pencilled letters beside them, none of which meant anything to me. Using my handkerchief as a wrapper, I dialled the first number, and found myself rewarded with the valuable information that the Farmers' Trust Bank would be open for business next morning at nine sharp. The second number I tried told me that Doctor Schwab was on vacation, but in emergency I could contact Dr Hart, number supplied. Juliet's system was becoming clearer. The letter B stood for bank, and D for doctor. There was an F beside the third number, but no reply when I dialled it. I tried the fourth, trying to work out what E D would stand for. Somebody spoke at the other end.

'Yeah?'

A man's voice, sounding bored.

'Who is this, please?' I asked.

'What is this, parlor games?' he snapped. 'Who're you?'

'Police,' I informed him crisply. 'This is the Seventh Precinct. Sergeant Kelly speaking. We found a man collapsed in the street. In his pocket there is a piece of paper with this number on.'

'Collapsed, you say, sarge? Who is it?'

Evidently the mention of the police hadn't exactly sent him into the screaming fits.

'That's what we don't know,' I barked. 'No identification. This number's all we have.'

He paused.

'Well, I don't think it'll do you much good, sarge. All kinds of people have this number. It's a public place after all. This is the Montmartre Cafe you got.'

That did not explain the pencilled E D. I decided to risk it.

'Is there somebody there called Ed?' I demanded.

'Sure. That'll be Ed Valentine. He's the boss. You want me to go get him?'

'No. That won't be necessary,' I decided. 'There'll be an officer round to see him. Thanks for your help.'

I put the phone down before he could argue.

The Montmartre Cafe. It could mean something. Or nothing.

But anything was preferable to sitting around with a corpse.

I cleaned up after me, and went out.

Through the door, this time.

NINE

The Montmartre is one of those places which is something and nothing. It doesn't have a phoney French headwaiter, and six-inch thick carpets to spill your imported wine on. On the other hand it also doesn't have a sweat-shirted wrestling bartender, and sawdust on the floor to spill your blood on. It's kind of in-between.

Take the guy behind the bar. He didn't have a jacket and tie. What he had was a frilly kind of white blouse, with what looked to me like black plastic sheeting wound around his middle to keep his pants from falling down. Montmartre, last time I heard, was in a place called Paris, France. The blouse and the plastic went with Spain. I saw Blood and Sand twice, so I consider myself something of an expert.

'Boss around?'

The bartender smiled pleasantly.

'I think he's entertaining some friends. Who wants him?'

'Tell him it's a man named Preston.'

'And that's all?'

'That's all.'

He looked me over carefully, then walked to where a small grille had been fixed in the wall, and spoke into it. The grille crackled softly back, so that I couldn't catch the words. Coming back to where I was standing, he said

'He won't keep you a moment. Drink?'

'Why not?' I shrugged. 'Scotch and plain water. Uncle Jock, if you have it.'

He produced it with a flourish.

'Newspaperman?' he queried.

'What makes you think that?' I parried.

'Your attitude,' he replied. 'It means cop or newspapers. I can always tell.'

'So what makes me not a copper?'

He looked wise.

'Ah. You'd have waved your badge. Always with the badges, those people. Besides,' and he pointed to the bill I'd laid on the counter, 'you paid for your drink. A cop would just have stared at me.'

The bar fraternity are usually among the world's great philosophers, and they don't make mistakes about people. This guy was a disgrace to the profession. Still, I reflected, what can you expect from a French toreador? Another customer saved me from further chit chat, and I looked around the place. There was a daubed mural on one wall, a street scene of outdoor cafes and cobbled pavements, with a villainous-looking accordion player annoying the passers-by. I made a careful note of the Montmartre Cafe in case I ever needed to make some French visitors feel at home. This was one place I must be certain to miss.

'Mr Preston?'

There was a voice at my elbow, and I turned to look at the man who'd spoken. He was medium height, thirty-five, and with a pleasant face pointed enquiringly at me.

'Mr Valentine? Mr Ed Valentine?'

He nodded.

'What can I do for you?'

'I'm looking for a girl,' I told him.

His smile was not encouraging.

'Isn't everybody? But you have the wrong place, Mr Preston. We're not into that kind of stuff. Try further down the street.'

I pulled out the picture of Juliet Freeman which I'd taken from the apartment.

'I mean a particular girl,' I explained. 'This one.'

He stared at the photograph, without expression.

'Why do you come here? And does she have a name?'

'Her name is Freeman, Juliet Freeman. Reason I'm here is because she gave me the number.'

'Ah, the number.'

He wagged his head as though that explained everything.

'And your name is Preston?'

'I already told you that.'

'So you did,' he agreed smoothly. 'But just a few minutes ago, we had a phone call from the police. All they had was the number. Something about a guy they picked up off the street. You wouldn't know anything about that?'

Ed Valentine clearly had everything screwed into position.

'No,' I denied. 'I'm nothing to do with the police. It's the girl I want to see.'

'H'm. Mind telling me what it's all about?'

His attitude seemed friendly enough, but the tone was edged.

'It's kind of personal,' I told him. 'Unless you're her lawyer, that is.'

He stiffened slightly.

'No, I'm not her lawyer. But I am her employer. I have a certain responsibility.'

I looked at him gravely.

'Employer? What does she do around here?'

He looked at his watch.

'Come inside, and you'll see.'

I followed him into the restaurant area, where late diners were trying to locate their food in half-darkness. The place was busy, but not crowded.

'Have a seat.'

Valentine parked me at a small table by the wall, and waved an arm. A waiter materialised out of the gloom.

'Get the gentleman a drink, Freddie. On the house.' Then to me 'I'll be back in a few minutes.'

He disappeared, and the waiter stood there expectantly. I gave up.

'Uncle Jock,' I said. 'And plain water.'

I was curious to know what I'd walked into. Valentine had been civil enough, yet somehow defensive. He hadn't shown me his muscles, but that didn't mean he hadn't any. On the contrary, he struck me as a guy who could handle himself, if he had to. Maybe it had to do with the girl. I didn't buy all that employer routine. It was far more likely that there was some other relationship between the two of them, the kind I could more easily understand. Juliet was a good-looking woman, and not the type to stay home with the knitting while Joe Franklin was otherwise occupied.

Somebody started playing a piano, and I looked over to where a narrow beam of light had suddenly lit up the far corner of the room. A very fat man was crouched over the keys, vast pudgy hands picking delicately at the ivories in a way that seemed incongruous from the sausage fingers. People all around kept eating and chattering, in that special display of bad manners which is usual in such circumstances the world over. I wished they'd shut up. I wanted to hear the fat man, as the magic fingers conjured up old images of other times, other faces. Then there was a new sound, a low haunting voice riding the melody against a background of blocks chords. The woman remained out of sight. All you could see of her was one hand, resting negligently on the pianist's shoulder as they shared the intimacy of the ballad. There was no amplification. If you wanted to hear her, you had to stop talking, stop banging around with cutlery. And it worked. One by one, the noises in the background fell away, and the only sound was that thrilling, sad-sweet reminder of times gone. The voice was low and searching, picking its way inexorably into every corner of the place, every recess of the memory.

When the song came to an end, nothing happened for a moment. People had to come back from those secret places inside themselves. Then, somewhere, a solitary handclap. Another. Then the place erupted into claps and whoops. The spotlight widened, and the singer stood there, smiling faintly.

She was Juliet Freeman.

I picked up my untasted drink, and sipped at it, as she turned to the man at the piano and said something. He grinned widely, and started off again. The place went quiet.

They did three numbers, or was it four? I was just as bemused as the rest of the customers by the time they took their final bow. It was only the sudden switching off of the spotlight that brought us all to the reality that it was ended. Almost imperceptibly, the noise level began to creep back up. I cleared out the last of the daydreams, and sat back, thinking.

Any minute now, I should have to start a conversation with the enchantress who'd just set me down from a kind of magic ride. How did I go about that? Did I tell her how much I enjoyed the singing, and then kind of slip in a question at the end? Like, oh and before I forget, why did you murder old Joe? It seemed to lack a certain polish, in the circumstances. Or I could get around to it more gradually. More offhand, I could do the bit about the singing, and then add in, oh, and did you know there's a dead man in your apartment?

There had to be a better way of doing things, and I was still working on it when a voice said

'Was that the lady you were looking for?'

I looked up, glad of the interruption, to see Ed Valentine grinning down at me. He knew well the effect

123

the girl's singing had on the clientele. Especially the males.

'All my life,' I assured him. 'How do you keep her?'

'Huh?'

He crinkled up his face in puzzlement.

'Well,' I explained, 'no offense to you. This is a nice place you have here, and stuff, but that lady needs a bigger audience. A voice like that could fill the Bowl six nights a week. Why does she stay?'

'Seven,' he corrected. 'She could fill it every night. And don't think they haven't tried. They've been here, the big guys. All kinds of offers. Movies, television, you name it. She won't have it. My place is right for her. Others like it too, in other cities. Says she's strictly a small cafe singer. In a bigger place she freezes up. Years ago, so she tells me, she tried all that big time, and it just didn't work out. Whatever it is she has, this is the kind of place she needs to bring it out. It's one of those things.'

I'd heard similar stories before, so I was able to understand.

'How long has she been with you? Reason I ask is, I'm wondering why I haven't heard about her.'

He nodded.

'This is her second week. She'll move on at the weekend. Never stays in one place long enough for people to get used to her. Maybe, if I'm lucky, she'll be back again next year.'

'Does she come on again tonight?'

He shook his head.

'Sorry. That's all for tonight. Come again tomorrow.

124

Oh, and I told her you wanted to see her.'

'Thanks. Do I go backstage?'

That made him grin.

'Nice of you to put it that way. Backstage, as you put it, means one crowded kitchen and a shoebox where the entertainers change their clothes. You put two people in there, you need a shoehorn to get 'em out. No. She said she'd just get changed, and she'll come out to the table. You're lucky. In the usual way she won't mingle with the customers.'

I thanked him, and offered him a drink, which he refused.

'Thanks anyway, but I have to do some mingling of my own. People like to see the proprietor around.'

He went away, and I settled down to wait. After five minutes, I started looking at my watch. That was normal male impatience. After ten minutes, it became agitation. What was she doing back there? Well, shoebox or no, I'd better find out. Crossing the floor, I went out through the swing door behind the piano. It was the usual out-of-sight chaos of a restaurant kitchen. A big man in a chef's hat stared at me malevolently.

'You looking for the john?' he demanded.

He was wielding a huge knife that would have been appropriate for jungle clearance.

'No,' I replied, with an ingratiating smile. 'I'm looking for Miss Freeman.'

If that was supposed to mollify him, it didn't make the knife waver an inch.

'One of those,' he answered. 'Well, you're too late,

buddy. She took off. Why don't you do the same?'

'Took off?' I echoed. 'You mean she's left?'

'That's what it meant last time I looked,' he said unfeelingly. 'Well, are you going?'

'Yes,' I assured him hastily. 'I'm going.'

A side door led me into an alley. I went out into the night, cursing myself for having let her slip away. I ought to have been more pushy with Valentine, when he suggested I wait. I ought to have – but then we all know what we ought to have done, after it's too late to do it. For a moment I contemplated going back inside and having it out with Valentine. What would that get me? A bland denial, at best. A fast shuffle from a pack of waiters, at worst. No profit, either way.

I wasn't looking for a brawl. I was looking for answers. The night streets were grim as I drove back to Juliet's apartment. At least, on this visit, I knew which windows to watch. I ought to. They were practically outlined in sweat. There were no lights showing, and I sat in the car, trying to work out what that could mean. Juliet had, at most, a fifteen-minute start on me. Scarcely enough time to have reached home, packed up, and taken off again. I decided to hang around, see if she showed. In the next apartment, the kitchen light had now been doused, so the lady chef had finished cooking whatever it was that had so absorbed her as I clung to that unfriendly wall. Even now, she was probably sitting in front of the late show, packing the stuff away. If so, she had an uneasy night's sleep ahead of her. Still, at least she had the choice. It was better than sitting in a car on an unlit street, staring at a couple of blank windows. I fidgeted around, peeking at my watch every two minutes. Altogether, I stuck to it for just over an hour, then I gave up. Juliet Freeman had either taken off, or she'd found some better way of passing the time. A man didn't need a lot of training to work out what that might be, and the thought didn't cheer me at all.

You could say I wasn't at my best when I started the motor, and drove reluctantly back to Parkside.

TEN

When I finally rolled into the office the following morning, I was a man with a problem. Charging up the clients with work done and legitimate expenses is one thing. Robbing them is something else. Sheila Fyffe had hired me to see if I couldn't come up with a murder charge against the man she thought had murdered her friend Honoria. I had done a little poking around, in an ineffectual kind of way, but it was ended. The suspect was dead. For me to go on taking the lady's money was out. So what was my problem? Simple. It was to find a reason for dropping the investigation. No one knew that Joe Franklin was finally out of reach. No one but me, and whoever finished him off.

When faced with an insurmountable problem, a man of high principles, such as me, has a golden rule. Stick your head in the sand, and maybe the problem will go away. For the moment I would find something else to do.

Florence Digby greeted me with her usual warm indifference. I'm going to fire that lady some day. She gives me enough provocation. The morning was hotting up nicely, and most of the people I saw were already looking as if they had taken a Turkish bath with their clothes on. Not La Digby. She looked like the lady in the ads, bandbox fresh, cool and elegant. That's one thing gets up my nose. Another is the way she runs the place, as though I'm not there. All that system and organisation, keeping the accounts straight, even keeping the Internal Revenue off my back. Not that I'm not grateful, but at least she could give the impression that it's difficult. Instead, she manages to let you feel that she runs the whole place with one hand, and could quite easily be doing a second job with the other, if she felt so inclined.

'It is Mr Preston, isn't it?' she enquired sweetly.

'Don't pick on me, Florence,' I warned. 'It's too hot, and I'm already edgy for other reasons. What's going on?'

'Not much. There's a missing daughter case. Sam Thompson has gone out to look into it.'

'Missing daughter?' I echoed. 'I hope the family understands the odds. Something like two hundred to one, last time I checked.'

She gave me that saccharine smile.

'The case has certain features. The girl took a few traceable items with her. One Cadillac for a start, plus all mummy's credit cards. And, oh yes, I almost forgot. She took the chauffeur too. That's quite a collection to hide. Especially once they start using the plastic money.'

Blast the woman, she was right again. She usually was. And that's another reason why one of these days—

'—and a Mr Valentine called. He seemed to think you'd know him.'

My irritability began to melt away.

'Ed Valentine? What did he want?'

'He wouldn't say. Just told me it was urgent, and that

he wanted you to get in touch with him the minute you came in.'

She waited, to hear whether I was going to explain about Mr Valentine. Let her stew, I decided.

'Get him for me, will you?'

I went through into my spotless office and waited for the call.

'Preston?'

He sounded edgy.

'Yup,' I confirmed. 'I want to thank you for all the hospitality last night. Unfortunately the lady took off while I was enjoying it, but I expect you knew about that.'

'Bygones,' he interrupted. 'Look, something's come up. I can't talk about it on the phone. Can you get down here, to the cafe?'

'Who's going to pay for my time?' I parried.

'I will. Listen, this is very important. Can you come right away?'

Well, if he was meeting the tab, my time was his, if you follow me.

'Twenty minutes,' I confirmed, and hung up.

He must have been watching out for me from one of the blind-drawn windows, because the door of the cafe opened before I could find anything to press.

'In here,' he motioned, leading the way.

We went into the usual square cupboard space which passed for an office in places like the Montmartre. My new client sat down heavily. There was a bottle open on the tiny desk, and it had seen plenty of action. Picking it

130

up, he tilted some of the spirit down his throat, neat. He didn't even cough. This wasn't the suave-looking character I'd spoken with the previous night. This was a new Ed Valentine, an unshaven, untidy, worried man. Or frightened. I wouldn't know until he started talking.

'You been nosing around,' he accused, 'trying to contact a guy named Lockhart. Mind telling me why?'

'Mind telling me why I should?' I countered.

He scowled with annoyance.

'Because I'm paying for your time is why,' he replied. 'And on top of which, I got some information could save you a lot of trouble.'

I thought rapidly. Lockhart, nee Franklin, was dead. Nothing that was said in this room was going to change that. The Lockhart/Franklin thing was over. The prime consideration now was the position of one Preston M. private investigator to the trade. Whatever story I came up with would have to be consistent with what I told the police later. I was wide open for charges of suppressing evidence, and Rourke wouldn't hesitate to nail me.

'All right,' I agreed. 'I'm trying to get him to let a friend of his late wife's have one of the little pictures she painted.'

Whatever he'd been expecting to hear, it certainly wasn't that.

He stared at me, slack-mouthed.

'Huh?'

'His wife used to paint these pictures, historical things. After she died, this friend, my client that is, she asked him for one as a keepsake. He gave her the heave.

131

My client is a very sentimental lady. She asked me if I couldn't get him to change his mind. Seemed to think I could put up a better argument.'

On a happier man, the look on his face might have been a grin.

'You were going to show him your muscles, huh?'

'I'm sure that won't be necessary,' I demurred. 'Just a question of convincing the man. First, I have to find him. He hasn't been at the house all night. You wouldn't know where he is, I suppose?'

For a moment, I thought he hadn't heard the question. He gave no answer, but simply sat there, staring into space.

'You're wrong,' he said, finally. 'I know where he is. When I'm ready, I'll tell you. It wasn't him you came after last night. It was Juliet. Now why?'

But now that I'd planted my story, the rest was easy to explain.

'She knows him,' I confided, narrowly avoiding the past tense. 'She was out at his house when I called yesterday. Knows him pretty well. Well enough to put him to bed when he'd had a skinful.'

His reaction to that was to glower.

'That don't explain how you got here,' he countered. 'How'd you find her?'

I looked affronted.

'Oh come on, Ed. I'm a very nosey guy. If people intrigue me, I like to know more about them. Following people is my life's work, you might say. Last night I had an appointment with Lockhart for nine o'clock. He

132

wasn't at the house, so I thought I'd come around here, and see if Juliet had any ideas.'

'And that's all?'

I heaved shoulders in that honest way I have.

'What else? And why are you making such a big fuss? Listen, if you think those paintings are lost master-pieces, you're wrong. They just have this sentimental value for—'

'Hell with the paintings. I don't know about no paint-ings.'

The interruption was decisive, and final. I sat silent. Then

'That's on the level, about the paintings?'

'Hundred per cent.'

'OK. I'll tell you where to find Lockhart. They got him down to the morgue. On a slab.'

I didn't have to fake a surprised look.

'Oh? What happened to him?'

'He got himself bumped off. Shot. Cops think Juliet did it. She's locked up.'

He was watching me as he said it, studying my reac-tion.

I said carefully

'Why Juliet?'

'The guy was killed in her apartment is why. Only she didn't do it. I want you to dig around. You're already involved. You know the people. Find out who killed Lockhart. The cops won't be looking, not with a suspect already in the slammer. If I don't do something, that girl is gonna get railroaded. Well, whaddya say?'

I stuck an Old Favorite in my face, and pondered.

'I'd have to ask a lot of questions,' I hedged.

'So ask.'

'The most important one is this. What makes you so sure she didn't do it?'

He tossed his head angrily, then subsided.

'All right, I can see you got to ask. Listen, if I'm paying you, that makes me a customer, right?'

'I prefer client.'

'Yeah, well, same thing. It means I can tell you things confidential, am I right? I mean, you don't have to go running to the law with every little thing.'

'Keeping my mouth shut is my stock in trade,' I assured him.

'OK well here it is. Lockhart got himself bumped off during the night. Juliet found him when she went home this morning. She called the cops and they put her away. She couldn't have done it, you see. She wasn't there all night.'

'So why didn't she tell the police, if it's that simple?'

Valentine clicked his tongue.

'Oh, she told them. Only she wouldn't tell them where she was all night. She was with me, and I got a family. That's the kind of gal she is. She wouldn't go wrecking my home. So you see where I come in. I have the ball. It's up to me to find out who did this.'

I looked around for some words that wouldn't annoy him.

'Let me get this straight. Are you telling me that Miss Freeman is willing to take this rap, just so your wife

134

won't find out what's been going on?'

I had to ask, because to me it sounded ridiculous.

'Hell no,' he denied. 'She won't stay dummied up for ever, and I don't expect her to. Once it gets around to courtrooms, and trials and stuff, then she'll have to talk. No. What we got here is like a breathing space. Well, will you do it?'

I would do it. The opportunity to stay on the case was too good to miss. Now that Lockhart/Franklin was known to be dead, I could terminate my contract with Sheila Fyffe with a clear conscience. I didn't share Valentine's confident assumption that his lady friend wasn't guilty. Joe Franklin had died before she started work at the cafe the night before, and I knew that for a fact. But this was not the time for me to reveal my hand. There was always that little charge of concealment that I was liable to. Indeed, if the public prosecutor was in a nasty frame of mind, he might even go for accessory after the fact, and that was a prospect which held no attraction whatsoever. No, I would use my new position, with Valentine as the client, to carry on poking around where I'd left off.

'If I do this,' I told him, 'I don't guarantee that you'll be satisfied with the results.'

'What does that mean?'

'I may not have any luck finding the killer,' I explained. 'That's only one reservation I have.'

'You got another one?'

'Right. It may come up that the girl did it after all. Had you thought about that?'

He shook his head.

'No, I hadn't. If she'd been going to kill him, she'd have done it a long time ago. Let me tell you about her and Lockhart. She was his wife, one time.'

I sat back and listened to the story. Most of it was news to me, some was familiar.

They'd been married five years earlier, when Joe Franklin was a small-time hustler in Atlantic City. Juliet was already making herself a small name on the cafe circuit, but she wasn't too bright where her heart was concerned. Then Franklin pulled some stuff that the local big boys couldn't stand for, so he ran off and joined the army, leaving her flat. It soon turned out that he wasn't exactly career soldier material, and I heard again the tale about how he took off with a lot of Uncle Sam's property. He never got in touch with Juliet from the day he first left her, but she knew all about his progress, from the law. Every time he pulled another stunt, the police would hunt her out, and grill her. She never knew anything, but they still kept trying. She had finally divorced him last year, and changed her name to Freeman. That had been a news item in the entertainment newspapers, and was therefore no secret. When she opened at the Montmartre Cafe, Franklin had turned up. He wanted her to go back with him. He had spun her a yarn that he would very soon be a rich man, but she'd heard all that so many times that she discounted it. Not that she was any longer interested in him, in any case. But, despite what he'd done, including the way he'd treated her, she still had this special place somewhere inside her for what had once been. I've met it before, and nobody can explain it, least of all the women themselves. But it's there. It had been there when she called *him* up, drunk, from the house the previous day. Against her better judgement, she had gone out to Montenero Drive, and that was when I had first seen her. How he had subsequently managed to get into her apartment, and who could have found him there and killed him, were matters on which Ed Valentine could offer no advice.

When he finally reached the end of the story, he waited for my reaction. Evidently I wasn't quick enough to suit him.

'Ain't you gonna say something?' he demanded.

I nodded.

'Oh yes. But I can't guarantee you'll like it. It's a good thing I'm working for you, Ed. It's a good thing I'm not some hotshot Assistant District Attorney. I have to tell you this. All you've done, these past few minutes, is to give me a first-class case against Juliet Freeman. Everything is against her. With Franklin being what he was, and taking account of the way he treated his wife, nobody would go for Murder One. But Murder Two? Open and shut, the way you tell it.'

'I can see where you're going to be a great help,' he said bitterly.

'It's no use our blinding ourselves to the facts. The law has all the advantages here, and we'd be fools to forget that.'

His face brightened a little.

'But you said "we",' he pointed out. 'So you're still in, right?'

'I'm still in,' I confirmed. 'Never did like open and shut cases. People can get their fingers trapped. Tell me, did Franklin give Juliet any hint as to where he expected to collect all this money he was talking about?'

He spread his hands dismissively.

'Nah,' he denied. 'He was always full of that kind of crap. Rich tomorrow, you know the kind of guy.'

'Did Juliet ever mention any other names, people that Franklin knew, stuff like that?'

Valentine scratched at his head.

'Not that I recall,' he admitted. 'You'd have to talk with her.'

I rejected that idea at once.

'No. I'm better working out of sight. If Rourke finds out I'm poking my nose into his nice tidy case, he might flatten it for me. The least he'll do is to warn me off.'

The man at the desk looked puzzled.

'Rourke? Who's Rourke?'

'Captain of Detectives, Homicide Bureau,' I explained. 'Nice guy, when you meet him socially. Hell on wheels if he thinks you're with the visiting team. Take some advice, and do what I do. Keep away from him.'

'Shouldn't be necessary. I don't go in much for homicide. Well, where will you start?'

'Damned if I know,' I admitted. 'I'd like to get a crack at the scene of the murder, but that's out. The place will be crawling with people from forensic. Maybe I'll take a ride out to the house. They were having the place watched, but now that Franklin's dead there's no point.'

'What do you expect to find?' he asked, puzzled.

'Who knows?' I shrugged. 'There's always something. An address book, diary maybe, telephone numbers. Bank passbooks, who knows? Maybe there is a sack in the roof with all that money he was talking about.'

My vagueness didn't do a lot to reassure my new client.

'Well,' he said doubtfully, 'I guess you know what you're doing. Keep in touch, huh? This is kind of important to me.'

I got up to leave.

'Look,' I havered, 'you understand I can't cover up for the girl? I mean, if she's guilty it'll have to come out.'

Valentine nodded wearily. What had started out as a few pleasant hours in the sack had certainly gone sour on him.

'Just do what you can.'

I went out, wondering what that might be.

ELEVEN

Sheila Fyffe must have been standing close to the telephone, because she picked it up on the first ring.

'Preston, Mrs Fyffe. I'm afraid I've some disappointing news. Our friend Mr Lockhart is dead, and so—'

'Dead?' she interrupted. 'Why? How? What happened?'

I told her that he'd been shot, and that a woman was in custody. She didn't exactly bust out with grief.

'Can't say I'm all that surprised,' she came back. 'I always knew he was that kind of man.'

It might have been interesting to know what kind of special intuition she had, which enabled her to foresee that a man was liable to wind up shot in the back. That would have to wait for some other time.

'Yeah,' I grunted. 'Well, as I say, I don't have any chance now of getting him to let you have one of those paintings. Sorry I couldn't do better for you—'

'But it's all right,' she cut in. 'Didn't you know? Whatever you did certainly achieved its purpose. I had one of the paintings delivered to the house not an hour ago, with a sweet little note from Honoria's sister. I misjudged that woman, I'm afraid. She said she'd heard I wanted one, as a keepsake, and she was only too happy to oblige. Wasn't that nice of her, don't you think?'

'Charming,' I acquiesced, frowning into the mouth-piece. My mind was a jumble.

My lack of warmth didn't register with her.

'So, all's well that ends well,' she chirruped. 'You just send me your bill, Mr Preston. I'll be only too happy to pay it. And I want to thank you for what you've done.'

I put down the phone, and pondered. It would be easy for me to read too much into all this. That's one of the hazards of the job. You can find yourself putting the most sinister interpretations on the simplest actions. Rowena Parker had not seemed especially interested in me, or in my story. The only flash of response had been when she thought the pictures might be valuable, and I thought I'd disillusioned her about that. Yet, she'd had one all the time, and promptly sent it round to her sister's old friend. A kindly action, any way you looked at it. She hadn't told me of her intention, but why should she? The idea probably hadn't come to her right off. She'd probably sat around, musing, after I'd gone. She'd thought about Sheila Fyffe, and how lonely she must now be. It wouldn't be much of a sacrifice to let the woman have what she wanted. It would certainly give Mrs Fyffe pleasure, and at small cost to the sender. In this world, there are still people who do decent things, just now and then. Why was I trying to make something out of it?

But my imagination wouldn't let go.

How easy it would have been for Rowena simply to tell me that she would be happy to oblige Honoria's friend. There was one possible answer to that which

141

wouldn't go away. Suppose Rowena hadn't confided in me because at the time she was in no position to? Suppose she'd decided the paintings were best kept in the family? Suppose I'd intrigued her with my chatter about Professor d'Agostini? Supposing she'd gone to the house and asked Franklin to let her have them? It didn't require much mental exertion to work out his reaction. There had been a flare-up, one almight row, and Rowena had killed him. She hadn't meant to, naturally. It was all a heat of the moment thing. Then she—

Then she what?

One or two small flaws began to show through.

In the first place, what was a seventy year old lady doing with a pistol in her handbag? It wouldn't match up too well with the lavender handkerchief and the smelling salts. Because it would have to be her own pistol. She could scarcely have asked Franklin to loan her one so that she could eliminate him.

That was in the first place.

In the second place, how did the murdered Franklin get transported from Montenero Drive to Juliet Freeman's apartment? Did the old lady sling him over her shoulder and carry him out of her car, then drive clear through town, and heave him out again at the other end? Of course, she could have asked a neighbor to give a helping hand. Even these days, people don't mind helping an elderly woman. But this wasn't a parcel, or a suitcase. This was a half-naked dead man, with bullet holes in his back. Minding your own business is a national pastime, but most people would be curious to know

142

more about the details, if they were asked to carry a corpse.

Maybe somebody else helped her, an accomplice.

Like who?

If I wasn't careful, I'll be looking for a mysterious masked assistant. I was going to have to face it. This new flight of fancy wouldn't stand up, no matter what angle I tried. In fact, running it through a second time, I could see it was more like the outline of some black comedy than even a half-way reasonable solution.

Frustrated, I got up from the desk. No matter what the theorists may tell you, not many crimes get solved by people sitting behind desks. You have to get out there, where it's at. Ask a lot of questions, punch a few noses. That is the way to get solutions.

I took a ride out to Montenero Drive. With Franklin dead, the police had no reason to post a guard. They would have removed anything of real value to an investigation, and so my hopes of finding something that might help me were not high. Still, I knew I had to look at the place. In the last few weeks both the occupants had died premature deaths, and that gave the house a special interest.

There was a car parked outside, a shiny cream-colored Caddy. I pulled in behind it and stopped, wondering what could have brought money people to such a modest address. Well, there was one certain way to find out.

I walked slowly up the now-familiar pathway to the front door, and leaned on the bell. Inside, there was movement, and then the door was opened. A large smiling man stood there. Behind him a man and a woman were trying not to listen.

'My name is Preston,' I told him. 'I was wondering—'

A pudgy, well-manicured hand shot out and grabbed me warmly.

'Jess Oakland,' he boomed. 'Very glad to see you Mr Preston. I hope you won't be offended if I ask you to take a seat for just a moment. These charming people are just on the point of leaving, and I'll be right with you.'

I found myself sitting on a chair in the small hallway, while Oakland went back to the other people. They were both strangers to me, but evidently important in the big man's life. He made enough fuss of them to give the impression they were visiting royalty. It made no sense. They were quite an ordinary-looking couple, and the man's entire rigout had cost less money than Oakland's hand-made shoes. He escorted them past me, urging and smiling them through the front door and back down to the car. He handed the woman into the rear seat with rare polish, and the man after her. Then he said something I couldn't catch, and came back to the house.

'Quite a coincidence, wouldn't you say?' he boomed. 'Those good people are from Oakland, only to find themselves dealing with a man by the same name.'

'Amazing,' I said, standing now.

He looked at his watch, not quite frowning.

'This is a teeny bit awkward, Mr Preston. I wasn't expecting anyone quite this soon. Naturally I'm anxious to give you my full attention, please don't misunderstand me—'

144

'I shan't keep you more than a couple of minutes,' I assured him.

'If they'd only telephoned,' he hurried on. 'After all, they knew I was here. I hate to rush these things. It doesn't give people a chance to give proper consideration. You've come straight from the office, I imagine?'

I realised I was going to have to cut right through all this good-humored rush. The guy wasn't really paying attention.

'Mr Oakland,' I said firmly, 'I think we may have a misunderstanding here. I haven't come from any office. I just came—'

'Not from the office?' He did frown, properly this time. 'You haven't come to view the house? I think you'd better explain.'

'You first. I'm here on business, Mr Oakland. This is a private house, and I find you and your friends wandering around inside. Would you mind explaining that?'

It must have been a long time since anyone spoke to him that way. He controlled himself with evident difficulty, took several deep breaths, and stared at me uncomprehendingly.

'I don't like your attitude, Mr Preston. And as to what I'm doing here, I will tell you. I am Jess Oakland, of Monkton Realty, and I am in the process of disposing of this property under instructions. And now, I think, it's your turn. Who are you, and what do you want?'

The Monkton Realty Company is one of the most important firms in town. That made Mr Oakland a man of some status. What I couldn't figure was, why they

145

would bother with a small house on Montenero Drive. I also wanted to know why it should be for sale at all. If I wanted answers, the first thing I was going to have to do was to placate this large man.

'Mr Oakland,' I said carefully, 'I'm not quite sure where to begin. I had no idea the house was for sale. How long has it been on the market?'

He shook his head decisively.

'I'm not discussing that with you. Are you from some other company?'

'I am my own company, Mr Oakland. But I don't deal in real estate. I am an investigator. What I am investigating at this moment is murder.'

That, at least, registered.

'Murder, you say? Whose murder?'

'The tenant of this house, for one. The reason I'm asking you about the sale is because the man only died a few hours ago. Somebody must have moved pretty fast, for you to be here today.'

The confidence was now seeping out of him, along with the bonhomie.

'Let me get this straight. Are you saying a man was murdered here last night? This is terrible.'

'No, no,' I soothed, 'it wasn't here. He was killed way across town. But it was last night. Maybe I'd better talk to those people in the car.'

It was his turn to say no, no.

'No, no,' he ejaculated quickly. 'Don't do that for heaven's sake. You have no idea what this kind of situation can do to property values. Look, I'm going to

146

have to sit down. Let's go inside.'

We went to the rear of the house, and we both sat.

'Mr Oakland,' I began, 'I appreciate this is all a bit of a shock to you. But it's just as big a surprise to me, to find you in the middle of selling the place. How did you move so fast?'

He was so bemused with his own thoughts that he didn't at once question my authority.

'Not particularly fast,' he denied. 'This place has been on the books for a week now. Not much call for this kind of stuff at this time of year. These people outside are the first who've shown any interest.'

I realised I was going to have to place my questions with care. Jess Oakland, unless I was a mile off target, would know nothing about the case. Nothing about the people involved. He was just exactly what he said he was. A man who was in the real estate business. Nothing more. But if the house on Montenero Drive had been available for sale for a week, then somebody had given somebody wrong information. The last I heard, Franklin had been told not to worry about being moved out in a hurry. Yet, at the same time, the property had been placed on the market. As for Franklin, well, he'd been moved out now, and in what some people might call an unseemly fashion. Oakland was watching me with some apprehension.

'Mr Oakland,' I began, 'I can appreciate that this news of mine must come as something of a shock. But I imagine you were aware that there was a death here, and not long ago?'

He wagged his head.

'Oh certainly. But that was very different. That was the owner's sister, and she died of natural causes. It's this murder business that's really bothering me. I didn't really want to take on this kind of stuff in the first place. Now, I wish I'd refused.'

'I don't follow that,' I told him. 'What's wrong with this house?'

He made a moue.

'Wrong? Well, as to wrong, actually nothing. Quite a good little house, sound construction and so forth. But the low end of the market, Mr Preston. Monkton Realty is a large-scale operation. We don't normally like to waste our time on these one-family units. Only agreed to do it because I was handling The Patch at the same time.'

I didn't hear the capitals, and the reference eluded me.

'What patch are we talking about? A patch of what?'

Oakland stared at me, to decide whether somebody was putting him on. The decision went in my favor.

'Not a patch of anything,' he explained. 'The Patch. The old Parker house out in the Valley. Four and a half acres of prime development land. Worth a lot of money.'

I wasn't listening as he went on to enlarge on his theme. I had done Sybil Fyffe an injustice. She had told me in the first place that Rowena Parker lived in a big old house. I had dismissed that as false information when I visited that lady in her apartment block. Then I recalled something Phil Page had said, the security man. He had told me Rowena was a generous woman. When I asked

148

him, just by way of conversation, whether that applied to Christmas, he had said he wouldn't know. At the time, I hadn't read anything into that. It could simply have been his way of telling me to mind my own business. But now, I could give it another interpretation. Phil Page didn't know what Rowena's Christmas bounty was like, because she had not yet spent her first Christmas in the place. What else had he said? I dug around in my memory for any scrap that might help. I remembered that he had been enthusiastic about getting twenty dollars for keeping an eye on things when she moved in. That could now mean, putting the two things together, that Rowena Parker had moved into the apartment some time since the previous Christmas. That too would make sense, in the light of what Oakland was saying. She wouldn't want the hassle of being pestered by prospective buyers in her old home. Since she clearly intended to move out anyway, the sensible thing to do was to move out in advance, and let Monkton Realty get on with their work.

'I'm sorry to be the one to give you the bad news, Mr Oakland,' I assured him. 'Still, since the actual murder took place across town, there's no reason why this address should be affected. Somebody ought to tell the lawyers, I imagine. The dead man was a tenant, after all. No need for you to be involved. I was thinking of calling on old man Prentiss anyway.'

That brought his head up sharply.

'Mr Prentiss?' he queried. 'Are you sure you have no interest in the property angle here?'

My surprised reaction was not assumed.

'Absolutely not,' I confirmed. 'But what made you ask?'

The real estate man bit his lip, while he considered whether I was telling the truth. I seemed to win the decision.

'It's odd that you should know that Prentiss and Prentiss are handling this matter, that's all.'

'Odd? How, odd? They seem to be handling everything else for Miss Parker. Why wouldn't they deal with this? Or are you suggesting it's supposed to be some kind of secret?'

'No – o – o,' he denied slowly. 'Not secret of course, but it isn't exactly front-page news either. No one wants to draw unnecessary attention to it, that's all. Miss Parker is perfectly within her rights in placing her legal business wherever she chooses. It's just that a few of us in town were a little surprised when she transferred to the Prentiss people. Wonderful firm, and don't make any mistake about that. Excellent people. First class, absolutely. But when someone has dealt with the same firm for over thirty years, it's rather unsettling to have them change horses. It – how shall I say – it rocks the boat. Yes, that's it. It rocks the boat.'

This was news to me, and my face probably showed it. I didn't care.

'Are you saying that Miss Parker only recently changed her lawyers? Because, believe me, I had no idea.'

He jerked his head up and down vigorously.

'Absolutely. Wagstaff and Brothers have been the Parker lawyers since I first started business. Like I say, it's her affair. Still a free country, in some respects.'

Jokes, yet.

'Maybe they had a fight,' I suggested. 'Old people can take offense very quickly. You said yourself it's a free country. And the richer you are, the freer.'

'I guess that's true,' he acknowledged. 'I have a couple of elderly relations of my own. Believe me, tetchy is not the word for the way they react at times. Look, Mr Preston, I really have to get back to my clients. They're going to wonder what the hell is going on in here.'

I grinned at him.

'But you won't tell them, will you? You'll probably say I've been trying to persuade you to sell you the house. You refused, naturally, because they were here first.'

Oakland had a grin of his own, and it lit up his whole face.

'Something of the kind had crossed my mind,' he admitted. 'I'd better go. I'm taking no notice of this murder business. After all, it isn't even in the papers yet, so what would I know about it? I have to lock the place up, of course. Are you ready to leave?'

'Just one thing I want to look at.'

I walked through into the bedroom, and peered under the bed. The boxes were gone. Oakland stood in the doorway, with a puzzled expression.

'Checking for burglars?' he queried.

'Last time I was here, I dropped my lucky piece, a

silver dollar. These things sometimes roll under the bed. Not this time.'

'Glad you told me. If it turns up, I'll know it's yours.'

We went outside. Two anxious faces watched us from the rear of the Cadillac.

'Looks like you might have some new owners in the next few minutes,' I suggested.

'Let's hope you're right. I've wasted enough time on this place already.'

We shook hands and he went smiling back to his pigeons.

I went off to find somewhere to think.

TWELVE

A good place for a man to go, when he wants a chance to think something through, is a crowded bar. He can sit in a corner, all by himself, and switch off the surrounding noise. Sam's is just such a place. Full of jostling, fast-talking men. A lot of laughter, a lot of smoke, and a lot of isolation if you choose to keep to yourself. I had to stand and wait while Sam dealt with some of his thirsty clientele, then he spotted me and moved along the bar.

'What'll it be, Mr Preston?'

'Beer.'

He pulled away at his old-fashioned pump, and set a glass of the foaming suds in front of me. Then he leaned over, keeping his voice low.

'There was a guy here, asking for you.'

Judging by the anxious looks he was casting from side to side, Sam was doing more than being confidential. He was being positively secretive.

'What kind of a guy?' I asked, matching his volume.

'Young feller. Looked to me like a C-O-P.' More worried looks. 'I never seen him before, but he said you'd know. Name of Henry.'

That would have to be Larsen, I decided.

'Did he say what he wanted?'

'Wanted to talk to you,' confided the near-inaudible

Sam. 'Seemed kind of pleased with himself. He said would you give him a call.'

'Thanks. Sam.'

I took my beer and elbowed my way through the crowd till I reached the far end of the room. Technically speaking, there are two phones back there. I say technically speaking because one of them is permanently in use by the horse-playing fraternity. That leaves one, to be shared around among the rest of the community. A little round guy in a mauve shirt and a yellow tie was speaking low and urgently into the racing handpiece. I edged past him to the commoners' phone, and called headquarters, asking for Larsen.

'Who wants him?' came back the query.

'Tell him it's Preston.'

'Calling him now.'

I heard some clicking, then the sound of a receiver being lifted.

'Henry? It's Preston.'

'No, it isn't Henry,' snapped a too-familiar voice. 'I imagine you're referring to Officer Larsen?'

'Oh hallo, John. Yes, he wanted me to call him.'

There was a kind of low growl at the other end.

'Well, never mind what Officer Larsen wants. Right now, it's me wants you. Can you think up a quick reason why you can't be here in ten minutes?'

I frowned. Rourke wasn't shouting or threatening, at the moment. But that didn't mean he'd forgotten how. In fact, by his standards he was being positively polite. The fact remained that he was still the boss man of the

Homicide Bureau. If he wanted me, he wanted me.

'Nothing springs to mind,' I admitted.

'Good. No arguments, for once. I'll see you.'

I hung up. Beside me, the little barrel man was working up to some kind of frenzy, and his face was beginning to match colors with the shirt. It would have been interesting to see how it all came out, but I didn't have the time.

When I marched into headquarters, the desk sergeant merely jerked a thumb towards the stairs. Evidently Rourke had left word. I went up and banged on the scarred door. Inside, a rather apprehensive-looking Larsen stood behind his chief's shoulder, as Rourke scrutinised some papers which lay on the desk in front of him.

'Ah, the aged deb's delight,' he greeted.

'Hallo John. Hallo Henry. And you can't have an aged deb,' I contradicted.

He glared at me, but it was just a routine glare, without malice.

'Around you, they get old quicker. However, let us not descend to vulgar exchanges. Siddown, siddown. For once, we meet under happy circumstances.'

By Rourke's standards, his attitude was positively fulsome. It made me nervous. I prefer him to be his own irascible self. Untrusting, condemnátory, an accusation in every glance, that's Rourke. This cosy, have-a-seat approach was unsettling. I dug out my Old Favorites and lit one, spiralling blue smoke towards the ceiling. Rourke promptly produced a packet of his noxious little black Spanish cigars and set fire to one. A thick cloud of poisonous yellow began to chew its way through the atmosphere. The closest beneficiary was Henry Larsen, and his face was a study.

'Don't you have a pipe, Henry?' I asked him. 'We could get a nice trio going here.'

'I don't smoke,' he said unhappily.

'He's got more sense,' grunted Rourke, fouling up another corner of the room as he spoke. 'All right, let's get to the good news. Preston, we located your man Lockhart, known to us as Franklin.'

I raised an eyebrow, thinking quickly back over the past few hours, and realising I did not yet know officially of the murder.

'That is good news,' I conceded. 'Is he in custody?'

Rourke looked up at his latest recruit and winked.

'Positively,' he confirmed. 'He is in the safe hands of the city mortician's staff. Nobody ever escapes, that's their motto.'

I permitted my face to drop slightly.

'You mean he's dead?'

'Let's put it this way,' said Rourke, leaning forwards. 'If he isn't, there's one or two faces down there going to look awful red.'

'How'd it happen?' I wanted to know. 'He hasn't had time to get sick. Not that sick.'

'Correct,' nodded the Irishman. 'But a man can get dead real fast with a few slugs in him.'

I pretended to understand now, leaning back and relaxing.

156

'Oh, I see. Resisting arrest, eh?'

He frowned, not liking the implication.

'Wrong. He was bumped off. Murdered.'

I was all perplexed again.

'So you have a murder case on your hands,' I muttered. 'Any ideas?'

He smiled then, thumping the desk with a flat hand.

'No,' he contradicted. 'We don't have any case. The District Attorney now, he has a case. You see, we already locked up the killer.'

If I'd been perplexed before, I was amazed now.

'That fast? Well come on John, who killed him?'

He beamed, enjoying keeping me on the hook.

'His ex-wife, his real one. Name of Juliet Freeman. All nice and neat and tidy.'

'Freeman,' I repeated. 'But that was the woman I saw out at the house. She told me she was a friend of Honoria Lockhart's.'

'So she did,' he confirmed. 'And that's what you told me, remember? I'm surprised at you, Preston. You think you're so big with the females, but it seems they can tell you any old yarn, and you'll swallow it.'

I looked suitably humbled.

'Well, just imagine,' I offered feebly.

'She didn't happen to mention it to you, about killing him?'

The question just kind of slipped out, among the general chatter. It was lucky for me that I already had a good grip on my facial muscles.

'Mention it? What kind of question is that?'

'It could have cropped up,' he said icily. 'Miss Freeman is a singer, working down at the Montmartre Cafe. You were there last night, listening to her. And don't bother to deny it, I have a statement here from a waiter who recognised you. Well?'

'Yes, I was there,' I admitted, looking affronted. 'So were a hundred other people. It's a public place, last I heard.'

'A hundred other people weren't trying to pin a murder on the singer's ex-husband,' he snapped.

'Listen, it was pure coincidence. I'd heard about this girl at the cafe, and I went down to hear her. I didn't even know her name. It was a real surprise to me when I saw her face.'

'But you must've talked with her,' he insisted. 'I've seen the girl, and I know you. You wouldn't pass up a chance like that.'

I shrugged.

'It's true I wanted to buy her a drink. Went looking for her, as a matter of fact, but she'd left.'

'But unfortunately, you don't have a witness,' he sneered.

'Wrong,' I crowed. 'There was a guy in the kitchen there, with a knife the size of a samurai sword. He didn't like me. He'll remember, because it was him told me she'd already left.'

'That's right, captain,' Henry interrupted. 'I spoke to that cook myself, and he remembered it clearly. It's all right there in my – in my—'

His voice tailed miserably away, as his boss turned a

look on him that would have crumbled stone. When Rourke spoke, his words fell like drips of ice.

'Larsen. Probationer Larsen. If you ever expect to grow up to be a great big detective, you are going to have to learn Rule One. Rule One is, you don't ever, not never, interrupt your senior officer when he's interrogating a witness. Not never. Nohow. Am I getting through to you?'

The unfortunate Larsen nodded, white about the gills. I knew better than to interfere. Henry had done me a favor, but in the process he'd upset Rourke. My own position wasn't sufficiently weatherproof for me to start meddling in departmental matters.

'It's lucky for you Preston that I have reliable investigating officers,' Rourke said nastily, after a few deep breaths.

'Don't think I'm not grateful,' I assured him diplomatically. That ought to satisfy both Rourke and his stunned assistant. 'Are you saying the girl went straight out and killed Franklin?'

'Not sure about the small print,' he admitted. 'We didn't get a doctor to the corpse till seven in the a.m. He'd been dead for several hours. Probably died sometime between 10.30 and 12.30 last night. But you know how it is with these apartments. Central heating and everything. Makes the doc's job very difficult.'

'Are you saying she slept there all night, with him dead, and then called you in?'

He peered across, trying to decide if I was poking holes in his theory.

'No,' he muttered. 'She was out most of the night. With some man, so she claims. But he doesn't have a name. Anyway, we don't need him. Franklin was her husband, and he was bumped off in her apartment. We got all we want. She even admits they quarrelled.'

I was about to learn something.

'Oh really? So she admits letting him into the apartment?'

It seemed to strike the right note. Rourke actually smiled.

'Right. He came looking for her. He knew where she'd be, because she always uses the same apartment block whenever she has a singing job anywhere within twenty miles of this city. Told her he was into some real big money, and wanted to get together again. It was the same old tale he'd told her for years, and he got the usual answer. Then, or so she says, she went off to do her stint at the cafe. She told him not to be there when she got back. That's her story, anyway.'

'And when she did get back, this morning, she found him dead, and called in you people,' I finished.

'You can see where it stinks, which is everywhere. Reason I'm telling you all this Preston, is so you'll know it's over. This crazy tale of yours, about Franklin bumping off his missus. It's finished.'

It was my turn to peer.

'You mean, it might make things untidy?'

'I mean it's finished,' he snapped. 'It don't matter any more. Think it over. Calmly. You came in here with this theory that Franklin might have murdered his wife. You

160

couldn't come up with a motive. There was no money involved, no profit of any kind. Quite the opposite. The effect of the woman's death would have been to put Franklin out on the street, instead of in a nice comfortable home. You wanted to dig around, and you weren't doing any harm to anybody, so I didn't stop you. But even if it had been true, the guy is now dead himself. That evens up everything, wouldn't you say?'

I wished I had more time to get my thinking in order. I wished I had just one more day to check out a few things. I wished – well, it didn't matter what I wished. Rourke was waiting, and the time was now.

'I've been digging around, as you say. How would it be if I told you what I found? Five minutes, no more.'

'What's the point?' he countered. 'The man is dead, we have the killer locked up. Or is this the one about the missing will?'

If I didn't grab his attention, he was going to throw me out.

'Try this,' I urged. 'Suppose Franklin wasn't alone in killing his wife? Suppose he had help. Then maybe the person who helped him could also be the one who killed him.'

It all came out in a rush and it didn't sound very convincing.

Rourke sighed.

'And who is this unknown accomplice. Does he have a name?'

I took a deep breath, and my voice was little more than a whisper.

161

'I'm thinking about Rowena Parker.'

The groan that escaped from the man behind the desk would have done credit to one of those graveyard horror movies.

'The Faro Queen? Can I believe my ears?' He looked up at the carefully impassive Larsen. 'Now, I want you to pay particular attention to what Mr Preston is saying. You might learn something. We all might. Please go ahead, Mr Preston.'

'Right,' I began, then he cut in again.

'Oh, and while you're listening to Mr Preston, just keep one tiny thing in mind. This new suspect is nearly seventy-five years old.'

Larsen's face dropped slightly at this new intelligence. I knew I was going to need to control my temper if I was going to make any impression.

'Never mind how old she is,' I said tightly. 'A womam is always a woman first and foremost. I think you might be interested to hear what that lady has been doing.'

Rourke shrugged and sat back in his chair. He had the air of a man who had let an idiot into his office, and would now have to bear the consequences.

'Go ahead.'

'For one thing, Miss Parker has been planning for some time past to sell up her properties here in Monkton. Did you know that?'

'No, I didn't,' he admitted, frozen-faced, 'and I don't find it specially interesting, even if you're right.'

'She owns a big place out in the Valley. Depending on who's around in the development business at this time,

162

the site is worth somewhere between ten and fifteen million. She also owns, as you well know, the house on Montenero Drive. That too is up for sale.'

'So the lady is selling up?' he protested. 'Where is all this leading?'

'I'm coming to it. Even since she had legal business, it's been handled by Wagstaff. But suddenly, with this big decision about disposing of all her property, she transferred the legal work to another firm, Prentiss and Prentiss. Now, why would she do that?'

Rourke clicked his tongue.

'Who knows why women do anything? She probably had a fight with Wagstaff.' Maybe he criticised her hat or something. You know how they are.'

'Then there are the miniatures,' I went on.

'Miniatures? What miniatures?'

'Honoria Parker has this hobby of copying old illuminated lettering. She was getting very good at it when she died. There were two cardboard boxes full of the stuff at the house last time I called. I mentioned to Rowena Parker that they could be worth money. Today, when I went back to the house, the boxes were gone. And a friend of Honoria's received one of the miniatures this morning as a present from Rowena.'

Rourke puckered up his face, concentrating.

'I don't see what you're driving at,' he told me. 'You said yourself it was you told the lady they might be valuable. What could be more natural than for her to get to her own house and take her dead sister's property? I'm beginning to think you're coming unglued over this.'

I shook my head, trying to maintain my cool.

'Natural, yes, except that she knew Franklin wouldn't part with them. The journey would be a waste of time, but for one thing. Franklin wasn't at the house, and she knew it. She knew it, because she knew where he was. At his former wife's apartment. That meant the way was clear for her to pick up the miniatures.'

A large knobbly hand was raised in front of the Irishman's face.

'Let's forget about the damned miniatures, please? Stay with this new murder idea.'

I bit my lip.

'I think Rowena wanted Franklin for herself. I think she helped him to get rid of her sister. She was already in process of selling up her property. Once the deals were through, they would have moved away from the area, and we would never have heard of either of them again.'

'I don't believe this.'

'Hear me out. Franklin wanted to doublecross Rowena. He wanted to grab as much of her money as he could get his hands on, and get back together with his ex-wife. But he was unlucky somewhere. Rowena found out. She went to the apartment to have it out with him. Juliet wasn't even there. They had a row, and she killed him.'

I got the last part out in a rush, before Rourke exploded. But he didn't. He simply sat there, staring at me in wonderment.

'If anybody else had told me you came into this office with a yarn like that, I wouldn't have believed it. I just heard you with my own ears, and I still don't believe it.

Preston, I've known you since you started out. You sat in that very chair, and some of the stuff you have tried to peddle me has been kind of off-beat, to put it mildly. But this. This is fantasy-time.'

I stared back mulishly, saying nothing.

'What I mean,' he continued, 'this has to be the craziest, the flimsiest tale I ever heard.'

'I knew you wouldn't like it,' I said doggedly, 'but it's the only answer that fits.'

'Fits? Where does it fit? And what? It might be made to fit this whole insane theory of yours, but we don't need it. The known facts are good enough. What you've done here is to take a supposition as a basis. Then you've piled a great heap of theory and surmise on top of it until you have an entirely hollow, fictitious case, founded on nothing. You have to find something to fit it, and that something has to come straight out of a fairy story.'

'Then how do you explain Rowena Parker's actions?' I challenged.

'Explain them? I don't have to explain them. What that lady does is her own affair. When did it become illegal to sell property?'

'I tell you—'

'No,' he bludgeoned. 'You've just done your telling. It's my turn. This whole thing relies on Miss Parker having set her mind on Joe Franklin, right? Now, I'm going to be generous. I'm not going to dismiss your story on the grounds that there are forty years between them. It's a repulsive thought, nauseating, but I won't rule it out. It wouldn't be the first time, and it won't be the last.

165

After all, there were twenty-five years between her own sister and Franklin. So let's work on that premise. Here we have Franklin, married to Honoria, but her older sister wants him. The way you tell it, they then eliminate Honoria, to leave the path clear for true love. Everyone is fooled, including me. Then, out of the blue, Juliet Freeman comes into town. Franklin, being what he is, starts to have new ideas. He'll get what money he can from Rowena, and take off with Juliet. Rowena doesn't care for it, so she murders Franklin, and leaves Juliet holding the bag. Now, I may have misquoted a word here and there, but that's the substance of what you just said, isn't it?'

'It is,' I agreed.

'Yes, it is,' he returned heavily. 'But you have forgotten the main ingredient here, Preston. The stuff that makes the world go round. The suckers think it's love, but you and me know better. What keeps the globe on the spin is money. The almighty dollar. You put enough of those bills together, and you move into a different orbit. You walk the same ground as other people, breathe the same air, but that's where all similarities end. Take Rowena Parker, now. When you take in her whole estate, she's worth probably twenty million dollars. Try to imagine what that means. Twenty million. Somebody in that position, when they want something, you know what they do? They crook their little finger. That's all. Especially with a character like Franklin. All this stuff about murdering sisters and so forth, that is for the birds. If she wanted Franklin, all she had to do was

166

whistle. She wouldn't expose herself to any danger, because it would never be necessary. Franklin would have been on his way to her house before she put the phone down. It won't hold, Preston. It doesn't make any sense.'

I knew that what Rourke was saying was no more than the truth. It didn't suit me, and that made it harder to accept. In this business, you sometimes get a gut-feeling about a case, and no amount of evidence to the contrary can shift it. I still had that feeling, even after accepting what Rourke had put forward. There was a false note in the arrangement, somewhere. Maybe I needed a complete re-think. Maybe my first interpretation had been wrong, and I would have to try again. But of one thing I remained convinced. The real solution was not the one the police were following. There was something we had all missed. Me, the police, everybody.

I went back to the office and sat around, chewing it all over. When La Digby announced my visitor, I welcomed the break.

'Come on in, Mrs Fyffe, I'm very glad to see you,' I assured her.

She was as thin as ever, but the worried look on her face had been replaced by an anxious kind of smile.

'I hope you don't mind my calling in like this.'

'Always a pleasure to see a satisfied client. I was delighted to hear you got your miniature after all.'

Sheila Fyffe nodded brightly.

'Thank you, yes, I can't tell you how pleased I was. So kind of Miss Parker. After all, we are strangers. I telephoned to thank her, but someone at the house said she'd moved. They wouldn't give me a new address, but I was hoping perhaps you could help me.'

'Moved, you say? I didn't know that. What number did you call?'

She opened her purse and began to rummage around.

'I have it here somewhere,' she muttered. 'Anyway, it was the number on the notepaper. Yes, here it is.'

She held out a sheet of expensive perfumed paper, with a handwritten note from Rowena Parker. The printed address was headed 'The Patch'.

'Ah, I see. Miss Parker is evidently using up her old notepaper, and forgot to cross off the address. She moved from the house a while ago.'

Mrs Fyffe smiled and took back the note.

'Well, if you wouldn't mind just telling me the new address—'

About to write it down for her, I had a better idea. I wanted to see Rowena again, but had no real excuse. Mrs Fyffe would provide one. Maybe I would get a chance to search the apartment. Maybe I could find the gun that killed Joe Franklin. Wild speculation began to build up in my mind.

'As a matter of fact, I'm going into that part of town on another matter,' I lied smoothly. 'It would be no trouble at all for me to introduce you two ladies. Then you can thank her in person.'

She wasn't too sure about the suggestion.

'Well, I don't know,' she hedged. 'She may not want a total stranger calling on her—'

'Oh, that won't bother Miss Parker,' I assured her breezily. 'A most charming lady. She'll probably welcome the chance to meet her sister's old friend.'

Phil Page grinned when we arrived at the apartment house.

'Don't tell me. You're for Miss Parker, right?'

'You got it, Phil. No need to call her. She knows I'm on the way.'

That was true. I'd telephoned her before I left the office. But I didn't mention that Sheila Fyffe would be with me. Rowena might have baulked at the idea, and spoiled my little scheme for gaining access.

I leaned on the buzzer, smiling encouragement at Mrs Fyffe, who seemed to be a little apprehensive about the coming encounter. She was patting at her hair, like some nervous job candidate before the interview.

Miss Parker opened the door.

'Miss Parker, this is—'

Beside me, there was a gasp, and Sheila Fyffe staggered heavily against me, clutching my shoulder. The two women stared at each other, heads shaking in disbelief.

The woman beside me croaked out one word.

'Honoria.'

EPILOGUE

I'll say one thing for Ed Valentine. When you're his guest, you're his guest. Everything was perfect. The food, the wine, the service. Not to mention the company. Hortense Mulligan had left off the massive horn rims she wore when she was being a lawyer lady for Prentiss and Prentiss. Tonight, she'd left all the legal trappings at the office, and just brought herself. She was striking in a red velvet creation that set off the sparkling green of her eyes.

'Is everything OK?'

Valentine leaned down towards us, smiling.

'Just fine, Ed,' I assured him.

'It's perfect,' Hortense chimed in. 'This is my first time here, Mr Valentine, but it won't be my last.'

He nodded, pleased.

'Always be a pleasure, to see a lady like you here,' he murmured. 'Don't forget, Preston, if you don't see it, just holler.'

He went away, and Hortense looked at me speculatively.

'Whatever you did for that man, he's certainly grateful.'

I gave a dismissive heave with my shoulders.

'I got his star attraction out of jail. Wait till you hear

her sing. Maybe it will help to explain.'

She looked doubtful.

'If you say so. It just seemed to me he was a little more grateful than that. As though he was personally involved. Was he?'

Hortense may have left the trappings behind, but she'd brought her mind along. Well, green eyes or no, I'd been to some trouble to keep Ed Valentine out of the limelight. His affair with Juliet Freeman was his business, and I wasn't about to confide in anybody, not even the delectable Hortense.

'That's just you, thinking like a woman,' I evaded. 'You'll understand once the lady starts singing. Well, here's to Sheila Fyffe.'

I held up my glass, and Hortense did the same.

'Sheila Fyffe?' she repeated. 'Oh yes, that was the woman who put you onto all this in the first place. Yes, here's to her.'

We both sipped at the wine.

'She was more than that,' I explained. 'She was the key to the whole business. If she hadn't gone along with me that day, we'd still all be stumbling around in the dark.'

She looked at me gravely.

'Mr Junior is very grateful to you. If the sale of those properties had gone through, the firm would have been party to all kinds of crimes.'

'Not knowingly,' I comforted.

'That only makes it worse,' she replied. 'If Miss Parker had been a newcomer, an unknown, the firm

171

would have taken all kinds of precautions to ensure her authenticity. But as it was, with someone of her financial status, there seemed to be no need. I still don't understand how that woman came so close to getting away with it.'

'The keynote was simplicity,' I told her. 'And it damned nearly worked. You would have to understand about Rowena Parker's lifestyle. Despite all her money, she lived a very lonely life. She never went out socially, and nearly all her old friends were dead. I think it must have been Joe Franklin who first got the idea of the impersonation. Honoria would have done whatever he said. She was so grateful to him for marrying her in the first place, that he couldn't do much that was wrong. She'd been resentful of her sister for years anyway, hated having to accept her charity. According to her statement, the question of murder never arose. The way Franklin mapped it out, what they were going to do was to cheat her sister out of some money, then take off to some other part of the country and enjoy it.'

Hortense was listening carefully.

'I don't know whether you know it, but Mr Junior called in a handwriting expert to check the letters he'd had from her. The expert said he could not have told there was any difference between Honoria's writing and that of her sister.'

'That was where all her skill came in. All those years of copying those old works had given her this ability to imitate any style. A little thing like an old lady's handwriting must have been child's play.'

The lady took another contemplative sip at her wine.

'She won't get away with this nonsense about the murder not having been premeditated, you know.'

That legal mind was ticking over again.

'Why do you say that?'

'It was all planned too far ahead. Honoria moved into that apartment, using Rowena's name, two months before her sister died. The jury hasn't been empanelled that would accept that as anything other than premeditation.'

'Well,' I conceded, 'you would know more about that than me. What she can't deny is that she went along with everything from the moment Rowena died. She identified the body, using Rowena's name. She attended the funeral as Rowena, dressing in black from head to foot. She wrote to Rowena's lawyers, terminating their association, and then to your firm, asking them to take over. That was necessary, of course, because old man Wagstaff knew Rowena quite well, and no impersonation would have fooled him. Mr Prentiss was a stranger, and he would accept that Honoria was who she claimed to be.'

'I don't think you'll find he'll be quite so ready another time,' smiled Hortense. 'He's introducing all kinds of new procedures.'

But it hadn't been procedures that tripped Honoria in the end. Nor police work. Not even the intervention of a certain gumshoe. What brought her down was an act of kindness. She had a fond regard for her old friend Sheila Fyffe. There was no way that Sheila could be given even the slightest hint of the conspiracy, but it seemed a small enough thing to her have one of the little paintings. A memento of happier days, something to take out occasionally, and remember. It was a perfectly natural and womanly thing for Honoria to do, and it wrecked the whole careful fabric. It was a matter for reflection that if Franklin had let Mrs Fyffe have a painting when she first asked for it, then the whole plan might have gone smoothly ahead. But then, Franklin was a loser. His whole career had been a series of incompetent crimes. Even at the end, when he had every prospect of coming out a big winner, he had to go chasing after another woman, and ruin everything.

'What are you thinking about now?' asked Hortense.

'About Joe Franklin. Some guys are just born to lose, and I guess he would have to come into that category.'

She nodded, her eyes sparkling with mischief.

'It's an endless source of amazement to me, what some men will do for a woman. I'm anxious to see your friend Juliet.'

'Not my friend,' I corrected. 'Well, not that sort of friend. She's about due to appear. You can make your own assessment.'

The lights were dimming now, and there was that piano man again, picking fastidiously at the keyboard.

'He's good, isn't he?' whispered Hortense.

'He's better than that. Not that you'd know it, with the noise those clowns are making. Ah, here she comes.'

The first soft notes drifted out towards us, and the magic began to work again. First one conversation stopped, then another. Soon, the whole place was silent, except for that intimate exchange between piano and voice. I looked around at the rapt faces of the listeners, and wondered what private memories were stirring, as the golden notes soaked into the atmosphere like warm rain. 'Someone to watch over me' came the sounds.

Maybe it was the voice that upset Joe Franklin's plans. If he'd only kept his cool for a few more weeks, the scheme would have worked. Still, I reflected, men have been losing their cool because of some woman ever since that first deal with the apple. Franklin hadn't been the first, and he wouldn't be the last. Listening to Juliet, and watching her weave her effortless spell over the assembly, not excluding me, I began to have an understanding of the way he must have felt, knowing that she was back. A man would have to be all kinds of a chump to let go of ten million dollars.

But then, some men are.

Wouldn't you say?